A FALLING FOR FABLES NOVEL

MINED IN MAGIC

A FALLING FOR FABLES NOVEL

MINED IN MAGIC

JENNA WOLFHART

For anyone who needs a little reminder to believe in yourself.
I believe in you.

AUTHOR'S NOTE

Dear reader,

I wrote *Forged by Magic* (the first Falling for Fables book) during a rough time in my life. I was really struggling with my mental health, and I used it as an escape from the world. It was quite different than my other books, so I wasn't sure it would find an audience. I'm so glad it did.

These books are cozy, light-hearted reads when you need a break from the darkness, with a bit of spice for fun.

Mined in Magic is the third stand-alone book in this series, however, you can read these romances in any order. I hope they make you feel as happy as they make me.

xoxo

Jenna

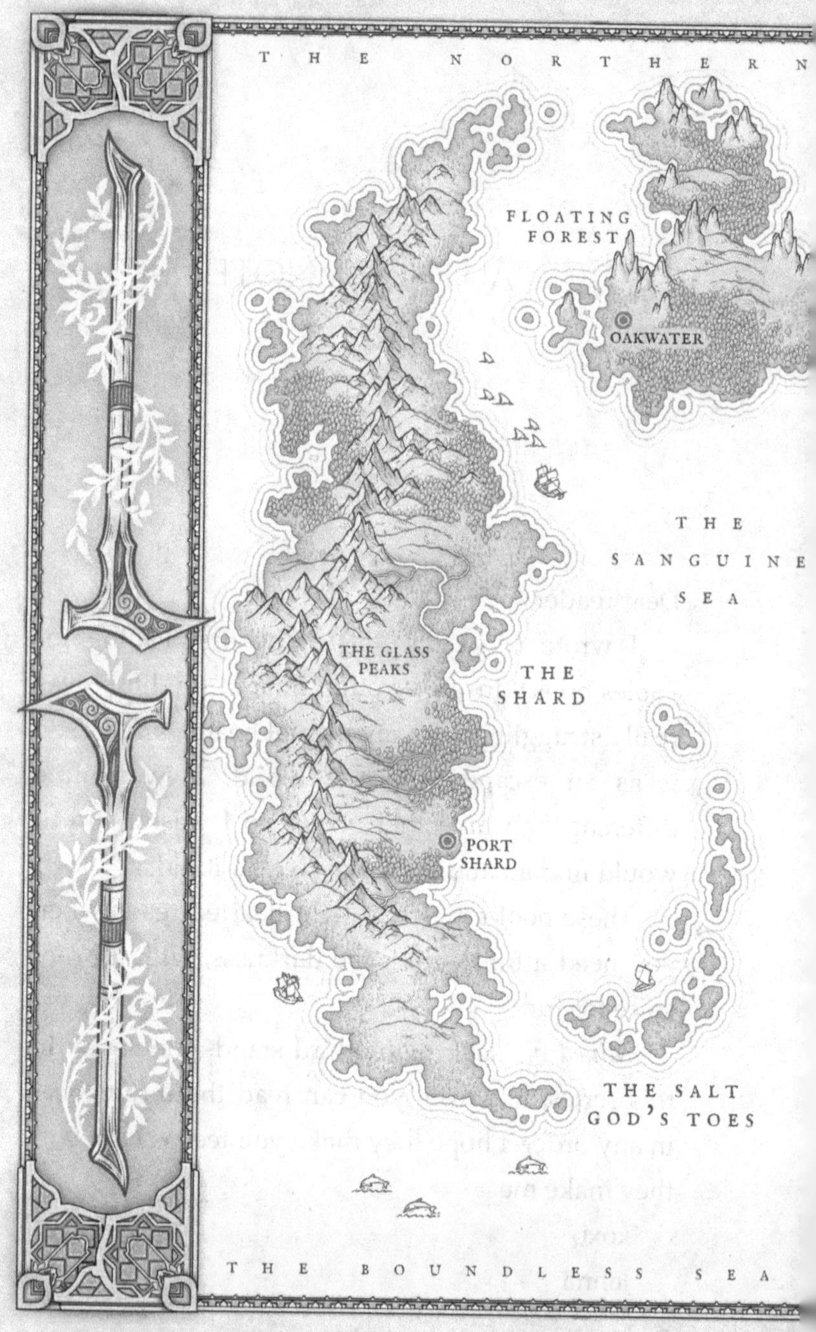

THE NORTHERN
FLOATING FOREST
OAKWATER
THE SANGUINE SEA
THE GLASS PEAKS
THE SHARD
PORT SHARD
THE SALT GOD'S TOES
THE BOUNDLESS SEA

OCEAN
THE ISLES OF
FABLE
RIVERWOLD
CASTLE RUINS
SUNLIT RIDGE
MILFORD
WHISPERING WOODS
ASHBORN FOREST
MOUNT FORGE
WYNDALE
HEARTHAVEN

I

ASTRID

Booming voices echoed down the mining tunnel. I lowered my pickaxe and rolled my knotted shoulders, bouncing my head in time with the lilting beat of the ancient folk song. At the end of the tunnel, around the bend, and two ledges down, The Wet Beard heaved with the dwarven miners who had already hung up their carts and their pickaxes for the evening. They'd traded their thirst for gems for that of ale.

Not me. At least, not yet. I'd join them soon. Because, according to legend, these mines hid a powerful gem, whose mineral traces wound like lightning through stone. Us dwarves had been searching these tunnels for it for so long, I couldn't remember a time when we didn't talk about it every day and night.

In fact, the song echoing from the tavern was about the fabled gem.

And I needed to be the one who found it.

It had power beyond compare. Of course, *exactly* what that meant, no one quite knew. There were lots of popular theories. One of my favorites involved endless amounts of the most delectable chocolates from the mainland. That seemed like a great power to wield. Who needed immortality or impossible strength if you couldn't enjoy something as sweet as cocoa? 'Course, as much as I'd never say no to chocolates, I needed the gem's power for something a little more important than that.

"Astrid?" a voice called from down the tunnel.

Hefting my pickaxe to my shoulder, I smiled at the girl who strode toward me. Her long silver hair hung down her back in a loose braid, and stars practically sparkled in her matching eyes. She wore a long gauzy blue gown and carried a foaming mug in her delicate hands. Fates, it was good to see her again.

"Lilia!" I beamed and hustled over her to her, careful not to trip on the cluster of gold-orange gems scattered around the mine's floor. These gems —sunstones—were still treasures, even if they weren't the grand prize. They glittered and shone, providing light and warmth in the dank, dark tunnels of The Deep. Without them, we couldn't grow our food.

Beaming right back, Lilia handed me the mug. Liquid gold sloshed over the edges. I took a long, long gulp, relishing the sweet taste. After hours spent mining, my parched tongue sighed in contentment. There was no other ale on the Isles quite like Lilia's. Not that I'd ever tasted anything other than hers and the brews found in the mountain here.

I'd been cursed as a babe. I could never poke a single toe outside these mountainous walls. The world beyond the mines would never be mine, no matter how much I wanted it to be.

"You're looking good, Astrid," Lilia said, bouncing on her toes. There was a new sparkle in her eyes that hadn't been there the last time I'd seen her. Squinting, I leaned in close. Blush dotted her cheeks.

"Hmm, are you going to tell me what has you beaming like a dwarf who discovered a new kind of mineral?"

She chuckled softly, and instead of answering, said, "How goes the mining? I looked for you in the tavern, but..." Her eyes darted around the skinny tunnel that vanished into darkness. "Still rarely taking breaks these days?"

I twisted my hands around the arm of the pickaxe. "What would you be doing if you were me? You can't even settle anywhere for longer than a fortnight. I've been stuck down here for twenty-six long years."

She sighed, nodding. "I'd be going stir crazy, too. Fates, I'd probably claw at the walls to escape. Any luck?"

I hefted my axe off my shoulder and angled the pointy end toward the nearest cluster of sunstones. "Well, we've got enough of these to light up an entire village. But as far as the Everstone is concerned..." Sighing, I dropped the axe heavily to the ground. It punched into the rock, the sound bouncing ominously down the tunnel.

"You'll find it," Lilia said, then pressed her lips together, like she didn't believe it any more than I did.

Shrugging, I started toward the mouth of the tunnel, letting the raucous sound of the tavern finally call me away from my work. "Maybe it doesn't exist, Lil. Could be nothing more than a fable. A lot of the dwarves have given up, you know. I've heard them whispering that it's pointless to keep looking for it. They think we should just focus on the sunstones. We've started trading them with some ships that come in from the mainland."

"Yeah, well." Lilia threw an arm around my

shoulder, walking steadily beside me. "We don't listen to naysayers, now do we? Besides, I've recently learned there are lots of fables in this world that are real. Impossibilities, even."

I arched a brow in her direction. "Like what?"

"Well, the dragons, for one." She beamed.

"Are you talking about your brother's dragons? 'Cause he's had those for years."

"Well, I have one of my own now." A strange smile curled her lips. "Two…in a way."

I tapped my ears. "I'm sorry. I think my hearing might be going. I swear I thought I heard you say *you have two dragons*. How in fate's name have you managed that?"

"It's a long story," she said with a laugh. "One I can't wait to tell you around a barrel full of ale."

I couldn't help but chuckle right back, despite my disappointment at going another day without the Everstone. Truth be told, I hadn't expected to find it. As hard as I tried, there were far better miners down here than me. If someone eventually discovered it, it wouldn't be me.

I eyed Lilia. "You bring me any of that chocolate?"

She shot me a mock frown. "How dare you suggest I'd ever visit you without it. I'll give it to you when we sit down for a drink."

"Chocolate and ale," I said with a nod. "Can't think of anything better."

Except I could. Clear blue skies, a sun beaming down on my face, and an endless stretch of world I'd never witness. But I didn't even need to see it all. Just one glimpse of the sky, and I'd be satisfied.

And if I could do it with a bar of chocolate in my hand? Even better.

"So, who do you think will win the Fittest Under the Mountain this year?" Lilia asked when she returned to our rickety wooden table with two pints of Balder's finest ale frothing down her hands. In our cities and villages scattered throughout The Glass Peaks, Balder was famous for having the best. His brew was nothing compared to Lilia's, but I'd never tell him that. It would break his big old dwarven heart.

I gladly took Lilia's offered mug and bit back a groan. "I don't care about that damn competition."

"Really?" She scrunched up her nose. "It's one of my favorites of the year."

"Every competition and festival on the Isles is your favorite. You love Summer Solstice in Wyndale, Yule in Riverwold, and you even like the

Harvest Festival over in Oakwater. Every time you talk about one of these things, it's the one you love the most."

"Perhaps. But I really do love the Fittest Under the Mountain. And *you* do, too. Or at least you did a few years ago. What's changed?"

I shrugged and scanned the tavern. The low ceiling curved overhead, its rocky surface worn smooth from decades of regular polish. Glowing orange gemstones were embedded in a scattered formation, much like the wooden tables surrounded by raucous dwarves. A few of the patrons wore metal pins shaped like a fist. Those were the ones who'd decided to compete in our yearly competition to see who could haul around the heaviest rock, run the fastest through the shadowy tunnels, steer the mine carts the best, and swing from rope to rope across the widest chasms.

All the usuals were in attendance. Galinn wore a cocky grin and lounged in his chair, holding court with the other hopefuls. His trimmed ginger beard barely reached his chest. He thought keeping it short helped him win, and maybe it did. Puldur and Knut sat with him, twins with long, bushy black beards and braided hair that matched. They were the two who'd come closest to beating him, but they were still no match for Galinn the Great.

That was their name for him. Not mine. I'd

rather go the rest of my life without chocolate than give Galinn's ego any more fuel.

Sighing, I turned back to the beaming silver-haired elf. "It's just the same thing every year, Lil. Same contestants, same trials, same winner five times in a row. Like the rest of my life, it's dull."

"Well," Lilia said, leaning across the table with a new sparkle in her eyes, "I met some folk on the road here. They said they're coming to compete."

There were always a few strangers who journeyed here from beyond the mountain, of course. Elves or pixies who wanted in on the action, thinking they could best the dwarves who trained and lived down here in The Deep. A few had given the regulars a run for their money over the years, but not lately. Every damn year, Galinn won by such a large margin that it was starting to feel like the competition was no longer a competition at all and just a way for him to show off his skills.

I folded my arms. "If I thought they had any chance of winning, I might be more excited."

"One of them looked like he could win, if you get my meaning," she whispered.

I arched a brow over the rim of my tankard. "Let me guess. Tall, muscled like the God of Thunder himself, and full of unearned swagger. He won't win, Lil. We get some of those every year, but they're always too big and heavy. This is a *dwarven* competition."

She merely shook her head. "He's got muscle, all right, but he's not one of the towering, burly types. You'll see."

But as if her words had conjured him, a big, burly type ducked his head and swaggered into the tavern just like I'd expected. He was so tall, his head skimmed the rocky ceiling even with his shoulders fully slumped forward. Long flaming hair curled around elven ears, though there was something very *not elven* about him—though I couldn't put my finger on exactly what it was. I sniffed the air. He smelled spicy.

If this was the contestant Lilia had meant, she'd lost her damn mind. He'd likely win the strength event but lose everything else. He wouldn't even fit inside some tunnels without getting stuck. And the mine cart? Forget it.

He scanned the crowd. When his eyes landed on Lilia, his entire body seemed to sigh. I sat a little straighter in my chair. Interesting.

"There you are," he said when he reached our table. The big, burly thing leaned down and dropped a kiss on Lilia's forehead with such familiarity that he must have done it a hundred times. *At least.*

I leaned forward onto my elbows. "Lilia…who in fate's damned name in this?"

A shy grin spread across her face. "This is Ragnar. My, ah…"

"Partner," he finished, sticking out his hand.

I eagerly took it, glancing between the two of them. They both had silly expressions on their faces, like two newlyweds. Two *very happy* newlyweds. I beamed at Lilia. It was about damn time. She was a wanderer at heart, always roaming the roads alone. I knew she loved to travel, but I'd caught a lonely look in her eye more often than she'd wanted to admit. And now she'd finally found someone who would wander those roads with her.

Good. Everyone needed someone who felt like home.

"Pleasure to meet you, Ragnar. I'm—"

"Astrid." He grinned. "Lilia hasn't stopped talking about you and your mining skills for days. She couldn't wait to introduce us."

"Ah." A flush spread across the back of my neck. "My skills are not amazing. Definitely no better than most of the dwarves down here in The Deep."

"Hush, love," Lilia said. "You're an excellent miner. And baker. Nilsa sends her love."

My heart swelled, even as a stab of pain went

through it. I hadn't seen my cousin, Nilsa, in years, though I didn't much blame her. It was a long trek from Riverwold to the mountains. She had her own life and her inn to look after. She journeyed here as often as she could.

If only I could travel to Riverwold.

"How is she? And Herold? They sent a letter a few months back, but—"

A hush descended upon the tavern. It was so sudden that my own words died in the back of my throat. Lilia and Ragnar both turned in unison, eyes sweeping toward the tavern's entrance. Three shadow demons with dusky, midnight-blue skin stood just inside, their curving black horns scraping the ceiling. They wore black fighting leathers and had small daggers strapped to their thighs and hips. Two of them—a man and a woman—were the big and burly type, like Ragnar.

But the one in the front...he was tall, but not quite as looming as the others. And he moved with a preternatural grace that defied logic. Shadows swept across his neck, curling in intricate patterns. He was slightly shorter than the others, but something about him sucked up all the space.

"Can we get some of those pins?" he called out, his lyrical voice echoing through the silent tavern. "We've come to join the competition."

2

ASTRID

"See?" Lilia said with a knowing smile. "I told you that one has something about him."

I nibbled on the inside of my cheek, watching the shadow demons. They'd shoved themselves into a table that was squashed into the back corner of the room. Two of them barely fit, their arms and legs twisted at odd angles. But the one—the unnerving one—relaxed on the chair like he belonged, despite being broad and muscled, just like Lilia had said.

They all wore the pin now. Balder had waddled over and had proudly handed each of them the metal fist pendant before wishing them Thor's blessing and luck.

And they'd certainly need it if they had any hope of not coming last.

"I don't like him," I said over my shoulder.

"You've not even met him!"

I eyed the shadow demon. He lounged there with his arms folded like he owned the damn place. "He has too much swagger. You can tell he thinks he'll win."

"Likely for good reason." Laughing, Lilia slid a bar of chocolate wrapped in golden foil across the table. "Does this help?"

Greedily, I snatched the treat into my eager little hands and hastily unwrapped the foil. The dark cocoa practically shone beneath the orange glow of the tavern. I took a bite. Liquid pleasure coated my tongue, and I moaned.

"Fates," I murmured, closing my eyes. "There's literally nothing better than this in the whole bloomin' world, and I don't have to venture outside this mountain to know it."

"I can think of a thing or two," a lyrical voice said, so close to my ear that I tumbled off my stool. My backside sparked with pain when it hit the stone. Narrowing my eyes, I looked up. The swaggering shadow demon peered down at me, his lips curved into a wicked smile.

"I can't say this is the first time a woman has

collapsed in my presence, but it's by far the most amusing."

I scowled. "Watch out. If your ego gets any bigger, you won't fit inside this tavern. No more ale for you."

He laughed—actually *laughed*—damn him. And before I knew what was happening, he'd wrapped his hands around my arms and hauled me to my feet. The warmth of his skin burned through my tunic. Scowl deepening, I twisted away from him and brushed the dirt off my backside.

"My name is Tormund," he said, like he was oblivious to my annoyance.

"Wonderful. Thanks for telling me," I replied, turning away and doing nothing to hide my eye roll.

A pause. "And your name is…"

"Astrid," Lilia called out rather helpfully, or so she thought. I just wanted the swaggering shadow demon—Tormund, he'd called himself—to go away now. At least half a dozen dwarves were watching us intently. The weight of their stares settled on my back like a mine cart overladen with sunstones.

"Astrid." Tormund tried out a suave smile, then motioned toward the bar of chocolate on the table. "I was wondering, could I try some of that?"

I blinked at him. "Wait, let me get this straight.

You came over here uninvited, knocked me off my chair, and now you want to eat my chocolate?"

"Uh oh," Ragnar muttered.

"It's been a couple of months since I had any cocoa," Tormund said. "And based on your moans of pleasure, I definitely want to wrap my tongue around a piece of it."

I coughed, my face flushing. Every word that jumped to the tip of my tongue died before I could speak it. Before I could conjure a reply, Lilia leapt to her feet. She tossed a second gold-wrapped bar across the table, and Tormund snatched it mid-air, reacting with the speed and grace of someone who'd spent a lot of time honing his reflexes. Hmm.

"Have that one," Lilia said. "I brought an extra for the winner."

Tormund's brow arched. "You flatter me. The competition hasn't even begun."

"You better prove me right and win then, eh?" She smiled.

I shook my head, promptly settling back onto my stool and whisking my own bar out of sight. I'd promised my neighbor a square of this, plus I wanted to ration the rest. Clearly, I couldn't eat it out in the open without risking losing it to a thief. And with my back now firmly pointed in

Tormund's direction, I figured he'd take the hint that I was done with the conversation.

He did not take the hint.

Palming the table, he leaned in, the light of the sunstone lamps glinting off his horns. "Astrid, eh? That's what you said your name is?"

"Yes," I said, keeping my eyes forward. His face was far too close to mine for comfort.

"Then you're the one who knows all about the Everstone."

I bristled. "And what makes you think that?"

"I asked around about it. Everyone said you're the expert."

Narrowing my eyes, I risked a glance in his direction. His eyes were keenly focused on my face, like he was trying to read my reaction—and like he was far too interested in what I had to say. How did he even know about the gem?

I frowned. "I thought you were here for the competition."

Down here in The Deep, us dwarves had tried to keep the matter of the Everstone to ourselves. We hadn't wanted word to spread to the mainland, where Isveig, the ice giant conquerer, had ruled with an iron fist. Isveig had been exactly the kind of person who'd try to take the stone for himself. 'Course, he'd been defeated over a year ago. And so some of us—not me, of course—had gotten too lax about the stone. Someone must be talking.

Tormund's eyes sharpened on my face. "Oh, I'm here for the competition, love. Worried I'll best you?"

I snorted. "Me?"

His eyes dropped to my chest. I flushed and crossed my arms over my ample bosom. "Excuse me. Eyes up here, or else I'll—"

"You have a pin on your tunic."

"What? No, I..." I looked down, and the glint of the metal pin stopped me short. It sat proudly on the right side of my chest for all to see. "But...I didn't put that there."

I tried to pry it off my tunic, but it was stuck there. And it would remain so until the end of the competition. Thor, the god who blessed this competition, didn't much like quitters. Once someone entered this damn thing, there was no backing out of it. 'Course, I'd *never* enter the Fittest Under the Mountain willingly. For one, I wasn't all that fit. And for two...well, I didn't care much about winning, except when it came to the Everstone.

"It won't come off. Thor doesn't much like quitters," Tormund said, repeating my exact thought, like he'd been reading my mind or something.

I scowled up at him. "*You* did this. You somehow put the pin on me. All so you could what? Keep me distracted while you hunt for the Everstone? Or fates, maybe you're *really* trying to get rid of me so I'm not a problem."

With my anger narrowed on Tormund, I was able to keep my panic at bay. Truth was, no one had ever died participating in the Fittest Under the Mountain, even if it was dangerous at times. But that was because no one entered who couldn't handle it.

And as decent as I was at mining, I wasn't even *close* to being prepared for this.

"There are far easier ways to get rid of someone." Tormund leaned down, palmed the table on either side of me, and levelled his gaze with mine. I swallowed and tried to shuffle back, but the table blocked my way. "My plan is much simpler. I'm going to find out everything you know about the stone. Then I'm going to take it *and* the champion's cup." His eyes dropped to my pin again. "Good luck with the competition."

He pushed away from me and strode back over to his table. The murmur of voices suddenly rose in his wake, and it was only then I noticed the entire tavern had hushed to listen to our conversation. Narrowing my eyes, I yanked at the pin again. The damn thing clung to my tunic like a cavern pond's leech.

"Oh, Astrid." Lilia knelt before me, her brow

furrowed. "I'm so sorry. We'll find a way to get this pin off your shirt."

I shook my head. "It'll never come off, Lil."

"Hmm. You might be right." She sighed. "Well, that's fine, then. It doesn't need to come off. You just won't compete. Problem solved."

But if I didn't compete willingly, the magic of the Isles would find a way to make me join. In the past, others had tried to back out at the last minute. Not once had it worked. Something always happened to nudge them into the arena. Quitting wasn't an option.

"Nevermind that," I whispered. "I'm more worried about him going after the Everstone."

Lilia pressed her lips together, then said, "Just don't tell him anything. How long have dwarves been hunting for it? Decades. He'll never find it."

"I hope you're right." Steeling my spine, I twisted toward Tormund's table in the back corner of the tavern. The other shadow demons were chatting animatedly, sloshing their beer and singing along to the bard's latest song. But Tormund sat silently with his back against the stone wall, his eyes right on me. My heart pounded. He lifted his tankard from the table and angled it my way, as if he were giving me a cheers across the room.

I lifted my fingers in a rude gesture and stood.

"Come on, Lil. Let's find somewhere better to spend the rest of the evening."

"Gladly," she replied. "How about your place?"

My little cottage was nestled in the dwarven village of Steingard, only three caverns west of the mining tunnels, The Wet Beard, and the cluster of larger trading shops. Steingard was home to about a hundred of us, though several families were expecting new additions which would expand our little corner of the world. The ledges that ran along the outer rim of The Endless Chasm were connected by arched stone bridges that curved over the looming darkness. Embedded sunstones illuminated the path, along with the steps that snaked skyward, linking our homes— stone cottages carved by dwarven hands.

It smelled of wet stone and algae and petrichor, laced through with a softer scent—perfumed flow-ers. We only had one flower that could grow here, a pale green daisy that clustered wherever we dwarves carved our homes, like the life of it was drawn to us. Someone long ago had dubbed them Daisies of the Deep.

"Steingard is mighty pretty," Ragnar said as we

walked past the flower boxes clustered on the ledge outside my cottage. All four of them were overflowing with the green daisies. I needed to get another box soon. Other than mining, my biggest joys in life were baking and gardening. Since I couldn't venture above ground, I did my best to bring as much life as I could to my little corner of the world. The flowers weren't much, but they were all mine.

"Thanks," I said, pushing inside my home. We didn't lock our doors under the mountain unless strangers ventured here. Several years back, a few trolls had raided a village while everyone had been watching one of the trials. Ever since then, we'd been more careful with visitors. I'd have to remember to lock up now that Tormund and his friends were here.

At the thought of the shadow demon, all the cheer I'd found during our short walk from The Wet Beard vanished like a puff of smoke.

Lilia and Ragnar took two seats at my dining table, the wooden chair creaking beneath Ragnar's weight. Lilia politely moved one of my moss plants out of the way, adding it to the cluster of eight others I'd collected in one corner of the room. Everything I owned fit inside this small space, except for my bed, which I could only reach by a rickety ladder leading up to the stone ledge just above my head. Other than the kitchen table and the wash basin sink, I was the proud owner of a new sofa built from oak and covered in cushions stuffed with goose feathers, though I'd have to replace it after a few years. The damp down here wasn't too kind to wood.

Just like most dwarves, I had my own stash of kegs in my kitchen. I poured us all a round of ale before joining Ragnar and Lilia at the table. Quietly, they both took a sip while I pulled out the bar of chocolate I'd stashed in my tunic. Right now, I could sorely use some sugar.

"What are you going to do?" Lilia asked, finally breaking through the silence. "About Tormund, I mean."

As if there was anything else she could be referring to right now.

"There's only one thing I *can* do." I shrugged. "I have to find the Everstone before he does."

"But what about the competition?" Ragnar asked.

Leaning forward, I waved the chocolate bar in the air. "I have to participate, that much is clear. But the rules say nothing about effort. I'll just live up to everyone's expectations of me and fail each trial nice and early. Some of them last hours, so that'll give me loads of free time to hunt for the Everstone."

"And Tormund will be too focused on the trials to notice you sneaking away," Ragnar said with a nod. "Clever."

"Ragnar and I can help get you more time," Lilia added eagerly. "After the trials end, we'll do our best to keep Tormund occupied with celebratory ale."

Ragnar slid his gaze toward Lilia and winked. "I love it when you get sneaky."

"To clandestine quests and cocoa beans," I said, lifting a tankard high in the air.

Lilia grinned and tapped her tankard against mine. "To Astrid Balstad breathing in fresh, spring air."

"And watching the sunset over the majestic mountains," Ragnar added.

Tears welled in my eyes, but I blinked them back before they spilled down my face. Instead, I whispered, "To friendship, no matter how many miles stretch between us."

And then I popped another square of chocolate into my mouth, hoping it would soothe the twisting ache in my gut.

3

ASTRID

The morning bell echoed through the mountain. I peeled open my eyes and rubbed my puffy skin, sorely regretting the fifth—or sixth—ale I'd downed before bedtime last night. Ragnar and Lilia had stayed for hours. One drink had turned into another, and before we all knew it, we were happily slurring our words and shout-singing our favorite bard tunes.

Now a rock in my head pounded the backs of my eyes, like someone was taking a pickaxe to it.

Ignoring the mess of tankards scattered throughout my kitchen, I rose and tugged on a fresh change of clothes before ambling out onto the pathway. My next-door neighbor, Yulla, was watering her flowers, her curtain of brown hair frizzing from the humidity. She paused and sent me a friendly wave, and then she froze. Her wide eyes darted to the pin on my tunic. I hadn't put it there, of course. It had vanished from my previous day's garb and had reappeared on this one. Damn magic.

"You entered the competition?" Yulla asked, her face paling.

"No, someone else put forth my name," I said, shrugging. "Not that it matters. I won't try to win."

Visibly, she sighed, and the color returned to her cheeks. A prickle of irritation went through me. I'd have the same reaction in her place. Me? Competing? It was a recipe for disaster. I knew that better than anyone. But that was the rub, wasn't it? It was one thing for me to recognize my inadequacy, but it was quite another for a friend to see me that way, too.

For a moment, I had the unexpected urge to prove her wrong, but that feeling quickly dissipated. The competition, the trials, showing off my nonexistent skills? None of that mattered.

Yulla leaned back on her heels, wiping her hands across her deep green dress. "Where are you heading off to at the crack of dawn?"

Down here in The Deep, we had no way of seeing the sun rise and fall, but we had a watchtower at the top of the mountain that provided a view of the world beyond. Most of us took turns up there, so we could signal the beginning and end of another day to everyone else. I was the only dwarf to have never done her duty in that regard.

"There's a tunnel I want to check out," I told her.

She arched a brow. "You think you might have a lead on your stone?"

"Something like that," I told her.

"You don't have your pickaxe on you," she noted.

"I don't need it today." I nodded to her flowers. Like me, she needed another box. "Looks like they're flourishing. Mind watering mine while you're at it?"

Yulla beamed. Flowers to her were like chocolate to me. She yearned for the days when she could get more than just green daisies, moss, and vines to grow in our underground village, but try as she might, nothing else survived. But still, she kept at it. Yulla was a stubborn little thing. A lot like me, I guessed.

"I'll do you one better than that," she countered with a beaming smile. "I got some new flower boxes the other day. Want one? I can move some of yours over to it."

"That would be lovely, Yulla. You really don't mind?"

"'Course not. On one condition. You got that

chocolate for me, right? Don't think I missed that silver-haired elf going into your house last night. And who was that hunky man with her?"

With a laugh, I lifted the gold-wrapped square of chocolate I'd set aside for her. "You mean this?"

She snapped her fingers together like claws. "Gimme."

I tossed the bar. It soared from my front door to her ledge, where she caught it in her open palm. With a wink, she unwrapped the chocolate and popped the square into her mouth. Her eyes practically rolled back into her head.

"So delicious," she said around a mouthful of food.

"Enjoy!" I twisted on my booted feet and traipsed across the bridge leading across the chasm. Wind whistled through the cavernous space, jingling the bells wound into my braided ginger hair. With a bounce in my step and a smile on my face, I wound through my little village and waved at every dwarf I passed. It took several hours for me to span the distance between the cheerful homes and the eerily silent mining tunnels three caverns over and ten ledges down.

I pulled a sunstone from my pack and held it aloft before me, my hand slightly shaking. This part of the mountain was so dark, I'd trip on stray rocks without a light to lead the way. Despite our overwhelming curiosity and stubbornness, us dwarves rarely ventured into this pocket of the mountain. No sunstones were found here. Only the rustle of scraping feet or the scent of rotten meat. Something else lived in these tunnels, and no one knew what.

No one except for me.

I pressed forward, my heart banging against my ribs. When I came to the fork in the tunnel, I stopped short and leaned against the cavern wall, waiting.

A tall demon with curved black horns emerged from the darkness I'd left behind me, the sunstone glinting against his dusky skin. Unlike the day before, he wore linen trousers and a simple black tunic that cut a sharp V in the front, revealing the hard planes of his well-muscled chest. Impressive. Not that I noticed.

"How long have you known I was following you?" Tormund asked, slowing to a stop and folding his arms over said chest.

I lifted my eyes to his face. "I thought I heard you one ledge up. Might have noticed sooner, but I'm not used to men stalking my every step."

"No?" His lips curved into a suggestive smile. "I assumed you had to scare them away with your pickaxe."

I flushed. "Flattery will get you nowhere with

me. I'm not going to tell you where to find the Everstone."

"Only because you don't know where it is," he countered before lifting his gaze to scan the forked tunnel before us. "But you have more information than I do, and it brought you here. Which tunnel are you taking?"

"I have no idea what you mean," I said sweetly.

"You came straight here after I confronted you last night," he said. "I know you must think it's down one of these. Tell me which one."

"And why in fate's name would I do something like that?"

"Because I'm handsome and charming, and you want to help me."

I snorted. "You are definitely *neither* of those things."

Except that wasn't *quite* true. With his cutting jaw and dancing eyes, Tormund was not bad to look at by any means. But charming he was not. In fact, he was the opposite—so much so that I would rather gnaw on a rock than tell him he was handsome.

But instead of taking offense, he just laughed. "Nice try, but you can't get rid of me that easily." He pointed down the left tunnel. "Shall I try that one?"

I shrugged. "If you'd like."

Tormund examined my face, his eyes sweeping across every inch of my skin—down my forehead and across my cheeks—until they landed on my pursed lips. Then his gaze dragged down the length of my body, like he wanted to memorize every part of me. It took all my self-control to stand there and let him do it. Everything within me wanted to waltz out of this tunnel and never look back.

I hated being in his presence, and I especially hated his stare. And his eyes. And that muscled chest he probably thought made women swoon. It definitely had no effect on me, and I had the urge to tell him exactly that, just to annoy him.

Basically, I hated everything about him, despite hardly knowing anything at all.

Finally, his eyes returned to mine, and I swallowed. "You're tense. I think I *will* be taking the left one, then. Coming along?"

"No, I planned on going down the right-hand one," I replied—as tensely as possible for good measure. Anything to confuse him.

He cocked his head. "Trying to throw me off the scent? Again, nice try, Astrid, but you're far too easy to read."

"If you say so." Without another moment wasted in his company, I turned to the right and walked into the darkness with my sunstone held aloft. I'd noticed he hadn't brought one with him. A shadow demon thing, most likely. I'd only met a few over the years, but I'd heard tales. They often lived in underground dwellings, like us dwarves, but they didn't light up the shadows with sunstones. They drew upon the darkness, fed upon it.

I shivered at the thought.

After walking for a good ten minutes, I paused and listened for the echo of footsteps. A faraway drip was the only sound, which could mean any manner of things. I hadn't been lying when I'd told Tormund I hadn't heard him until we'd nearly reached these tunnels. He was far stealthier than any dwarf, which meant he could still be lurking somewhere behind me.

But I had a hunch he'd taken the bait.

I smiled, retraced my steps, and made the return trek to Steingard. Tormund never once appeared behind me again. He'd probably found what lurked in those tunnels. Or they had found him.

Good.

That would teach him to follow me around.

When I reached the bridge, I spotted Jostein waiting for me on my front stoop with a basket of moss cakes hanging from his beefy arm. My stomach growled in anticipation. I'd been in such a hurry to trick Tormund into following me to that tunnel that I'd forgotten to break my fast, a mistake I'd not made once in my twenty-six years. We spent so many long hours sweating away in the mines that it was unheard of to miss a meal.

"Heard what happened. Thought you might be in the mood for some cake," Jostein called out across the chasm, brushing back his white-streaked hair, so long it tangled with his bouncy beard. The cavernous wind snapped his words and tossed them across the village.

Jostein was one of the keepers of the mountain, and he led the competition every year. He was also one of my oldest friends and had become something of a father to me since mine had died the year I was born. He'd always looked out for me. Poor thing was likely worried I'd hurt myself in the trials, and he'd come to make sure I had no illusions of winning.

"I'm always in the mood for cake," I called back with a smile.

He arched a brow as I crossed the bridge and joined him by my door. "I thought you'd be more upset than this. If anything, you seem…pleased? Did you want to enter?"

"'Course I didn't want to enter." I swatted his arm. "But the way I see it, there's nothing I can do to change it, so I might as well make the best of my situation. Since I can't see the sunshine, I have to *be* the sunshine."

Jostein chuckled. "You and your sunshine obsession. Would it help if I told you it's not all it's cracked up to be?"

"Sunshine? Or the whole bloomin' world?"

"Take your pick." He reached into his basket and extracted a cake. "Down here, we have everything we need. Warmth, light, and water, of course. But we also have each other. The best damn community there ever was, if you ask me. You don't need to travel the world to find something better than us."

I took his offered cake. The warmth of it soothed the chilly ache in my hands. "I know that. I'm not like Lilia, Jostein. She loves to wander. Her feet will always itch to roam. Mine don't. I just…"

"Want to see the sun," he finished for me.

"Yeah," I said softly, then cleared my throat. "But right now, what I really want is to eat this moss cake. Is it your usual recipe?"

He nodded enthusiastically. "Beet sugar, rum,

stalagmite milk, eggs, and cave wheat flour. And moss, of course."

"My mouth is watering already. Can't wait to have one."

He passed the basket to me. "Take the whole lot of them. Eat up. You're going to need the energy for these trials."

"I won't be trying that hard, but thank you. I'll never say no to moss cakes."

"Well, I'll still be right in front to cheer you on tonight."

I lowered my arm, and the basket hit my thigh. "Tonight?"

His brow furrowed. "Didn't you know that's when it starts? It's all anyone has been talking about for weeks."

"I've been focused on finding the Everstone. I had no intention of even watching this year's trials."

Lips set into a straight line, he plucked a moss cake from the basket and handed it to me. "You best get eating, then."

4

TORMUND

It only took a few moments for me to realize Astrid had played a trick on me, clever little thing. And if it weren't for the human-sized spider blocking my path, I might have appreciated the cunning strategy. Even if I made it past the creature, I clearly wouldn't find the Everstone in this tunnel. It wasn't here. It never had been. All this? It was nothing more than a trap.

"Be gone," I said to the spider. His pincers clicked, his bulbous yellow eyes luminous yet cold, like distant snow-capped mountains lit by morning sunlight. Beautiful and majestic, but deadly if one wasn't careful.

I sighed heavily when the creature didn't move.

"I have no plans to continue forward. Be gone, and I'll return from whence I came."

The pincers snapped.

"I have some chocolate," I tried. "Would you like a piece?"

As eager as I'd been to get my hands on a bar of chocolate, I'd only eaten two of the twelve squares, leaving the rest to enjoy in the evenings after the trials. I hated to part with one now, but it was far better to lose a square of chocolate than a horn.

His pincers stilled. I took that to mean he'd gladly accept my offer of peace. Raising one hand before me, I reached into my pocket and snapped off a square of chocolate. Then I gently dropped it on the ground and backed away.

The spider lunged for it, his pincers snapping wildly. I took the opportunity to back down the length of the tunnel and return to where I'd last seen Astrid. There was no sign of her now, of course. She'd be long gone, and I had a pretty good suspicion the path on the right would no sooner lead me to the Everstone than the left one had. In fact, I wouldn't be shocked to find more spiders down in its depths.

With a slight smile, I followed the path toward Steingard.

I 'd never before seen a dwarven village, at least not one like this. Bright green daisies bloomed in flower boxes and lined every stone bridge that curved from one side of the chasm to the next, and the persistent—yet gentle—wind carried their fragrant scent. Sunstones were embedded along every ledge, lighting up the gloomy darkness. They even emitted a faint heat that seeped into my skin as I strode toward the stone cottages. Despite the looming chasm, Steingard felt more like a seaside haven than a damp mining cave.

It made my bones ache for home, even though Azraak was nothing like this. Underground? Yes. Cozy and welcoming? Not even a little.

As I crossed the bridge over the chasm, my gaze immediately found Astrid sitting on her stoop and nibbling on a vibrant green cake. She didn't notice me at first. Her eyes were distant, like she was deep in thought. Perhaps she was imagining her little spider friend gobbling me up so I couldn't find the Everstone first.

But there was something wistful in her expression. *Longing,* I thought. I'd felt that emotion deep in my gut so often that I understood it for what it was. And there was a watery sheen to her eyes, like she was barely holding tears at bay. I slowed my steps. Perhaps I should turn around and confront her another time. She might be my rival in every regard, but I'd never want to make her cry.

But then she stiffened, and her head snapped up. An expression of shock rolled like a wave across her face, then she quickly covered it up with a scowl. Ha! She hadn't expected me to escape so easily.

I quirked my lips and strode toward her, my eyes drawn to her curves as she stood and brushed the crumbs from her trousers. Her thick thighs were to die for—or they would be, if she didn't currently stand in the way of everything I wanted. I rolled back my shoulders. *Ignore the thighs.*

"Overgrown spiders," I said when I reached her front stoop. "It was a good idea, though I'll admit I'm surprised. I thought the dwarves of The Glass Peaks were peaceful folk. You *are* part of the Isles the last time I checked, and they're famous for being a haven from violence and all things rotten in this bloody world."

"I'll remind you that it was *your* choice to go down that tunnel, not mine. In fact, I went in the opposite direction."

"And you wouldn't have felt even a flicker of guilt if the thing had killed me."

She laughed. It was a light, tinkling sound that jingled like the bells she wore in her hair, echoing all around us. Her eyes crinkled in the corners.

Rose dusted her cheeks. Fate be damned, she looked beautiful like that. If I were a different sort of man with a different sort of goal, I could see how I might be tempted to do anything in my power to get her to laugh like that again. But I wasn't. Even if she wasn't my rival, I could never get involved.

And so I ignored her beauty and cocked a brow. "The idea of my death is funny, eh?"

"I'm just surprised that a muscly, cocky competitor would be afraid of a little old spider."

"Muscly? Did you just give me a compliment?" I took a step closer, grinning. "That might just make up for your attempt to kill me."

"Oh, trust me. That's not a compliment." She cocked her head, looking up at me. "And Daisy never would have killed you. He's pretty tame. All you have to do is give him some folk food, and he goes on his merry way."

"Ah." I nodded. "That explains his eagerness to eat my chocolate."

Her smile slipped. "Don't tell me you wasted that cocoa on a spider."

"I thought he was going to eat me. Giving up the chocolate seemed like the better option at the time."

She rolled her eyes and threw up her hands. "See? You know nothing about these dwarven lands. And I bet you think you'll win Fittest Under the Mountain despite it."

"Think it? No." My smile widened. "I know I'll win."

"I have truly never met anyone with a bigger ego than yours, and that's saying something," she said flatly.

"If I don't believe in myself, why would anyone else?" I shrugged. "I learned a long time ago I have to back myself in everything I do. Which is why…" I leaned in and snatched a cake from her basket. "…I'm also going to find the Everstone."

"Not if I have anything to do with it," she snapped.

"Why do you want it so badly? As far as I can tell, no one else seems that bothered by it anymore. No one but you."

"I could ask you the same question."

I chuckled.

"If you're not going to tell me, give me back my cake." She reached for the green morsel, but I held it over my horns and out of her reach. Glowering, she folded her arms.

"Tell me where you think the Everstone is, and I'll gladly give you this weird glowing thing you call food."

"It's really quite tasty," she countered.

"Somehow, I doubt that," I replied, holding the

thing before me. Up close, it did look like cake, but it was hard to ignore the very vibrant green of it. "It looks like grass."

She sighed and turned away. "Right. Grass."

I frowned as she opened the door and shuffled into her cave cottage. For a moment, I hesitated, dumbstruck by her sudden change in attitude. She was no longer the annoying miner who'd tried to send me into the pincers of an oversized spider and was back to the girl who'd sat on her stoop, nearly crying.

As if driven forward out of their own volition, my feet followed Astrid inside, and my horns scraped the low stone ceiling. Astrid plopped down at a tiny wooden table in the center of the room. Moss, vines, and flowers consumed the entire space, blooming from the walls and climbing through the cracks around the window frames. I stepped past it all—careful not to crush anything— and joined her at the table. She didn't even look up when the chair creaked.

"Why in fate's name does grass make you so sad? You seem to love greenery." I gestured around her small yet comfortable home. "And if you don't, I have bad news for you. There are plants *every-where* in your house. In fact, I think they're taking over, and I doubt you'll ever get rid of them all. Might be time to move."

She sighed again and shoved an entire cake into her mouth. For a moment, silence descended as she chewed. A few crumbs dropped to the table, and she brushed them aside absentmindedly, that faraway look in her eyes again.

When she finished eating the moss cake, she said, "I'm afraid I can't tell you. But you should know it's why I'm hunting the Everstone."

"Ah. Right. Of course you won't tell me a damn thing. That would make things far too easy."

"No, I mean, I *really* can't tell you."

"Yes, I realize that. You see me as a stranger from another land who is trying to steal your prize and—"

"No, I quite literally can't speak of it. I can dance around it, of course, but I can't say the words directly." She shrugged, pulled out another cake, and then waved it around. Crumbs sprayed the wall. "It's part of the whole *thing*."

I sat up a little straighter. Back in my homeland, curses happened often enough that I understood the signs. The trouble was, we were not in my homeland. We were in the Isles, where this kind of thing wasn't supposed to happen. I didn't even know witches came here.

"You're cursed," I said.

She squinted at me. "How did you know that?"

I let out a hollow laugh. "This isn't my first

encounter with a cursed woman. How did it happen?"

Her gaze narrowed. "I don't think I like that term."

"What term? Cursed woman? I might as well say it how it is, even if you can't."

"It just sounds so…" She wrinkled her nose.

"Interesting? Oh yes, I agree. You have a curse, and you need the Everstone to break it. And I'm here to throw a wrench into your plans. Quite the quandary you have there. No wonder you sent me straight into the jaws of that beast."

She folded her arms and glared at me. "You're getting way too much amusement out of this."

I grinned at her. But inside, my heart twisted. Truth was, I felt for the girl. Curses were nasty little things, and there was no telling what kind of turmoil this one caused her. No wonder she was so determined to find the Everstone. Its power was great enough to free her from whatever magical bonds were wrapped around her wrists. For a moment, I actually considered walking away from all of it.

But I couldn't let myself think like that. Astrid looked well enough. She had a roof over her head, plenty of food, and friends to keep her company. Empathy was dangerous. It would make me hesitate when I needed to move forward with fierce determination.

"I've had enough. You can go now," she said. "And don't let the door hit your arse on the way out."

I widened my smile to hide my thoughts. "My muscled arse, according to you."

"You are the most insufferable man I've ever met. Has anyone ever told you that?"

"*Demon.* And I appreciate the compliment. It's the second one you've gifted me."

She groaned. "Get out, Tormund. That is a *bound order.*"

Magic seized me by the back of the neck and tugged me to my feet. And then it started dragging me toward Astrid's open door. Before I got too far away from the table, I snatched one of those moss cakes from the basket. As disgusting as they looked, I had to show the others.

"Surprised you know how to get rid of a shadow demon," I called over my shoulder.

"Good. I hope you keep underestimating me. It'll make it far more satisfying when I beat you."

"At the competition or to the Everstone?" Magic heaved me out onto her stoop and dropped me there. Bloody bound orders. When the goddess Freya gave shadow demons this weakness, I didn't think she intended it to be used this way. It was supposed to keep humans safe at night from those of us who used our allure to tempt them into bed. Instead, Astrid, who was very much *not* human and not being tempted, was doing it to make a point.

Astrid smiled serenely from her kitchen table. "You'll find out soon enough."

And with that, a gust of wind slammed the door in my face, and the lock tumbled shut.

5

ASTRID

"I shouldn't have said that to him," I whispered into Lilia's ear, her silver hair parting around the curved tip. "Now he's going to expect a grand show from me during the competition, and if I don't give it to him, he'll be all smug and annoying about it."

Lilia slung an arm around my shoulder and steered me toward the arena inside one of our many Great Halls, the ceiling so high that I could barely see it. My boots scuffed the cavern floor. The last thing I wanted to do right now was walk before the crowd cheering in the stands that circled the pit. All the other competitors were inside, as far as I could tell. And the dwarven cheers were loud enough to wake the bloomin' dead.

I'd have to walk into the arena with all eyes on

me, the *cursed woman* who'd been entered against her will.

"Just forget about Tormund for now and have fun!" Lilia led me toward the arched stone gate, where dozens of bells hung from colorful ribbons, jingling in the breeze. "This is only for a laugh. You don't actually have to do well, remember?"

Except Tormund would expect I'd try. And if I failed miserably, not only would he look at me with an annoying laughing smirk, but his cockiness about the Everstone would grow five sizes larger. I didn't know how much more of his ego I could take. I could already see the twinkle in his eyes, bright enough to light up a cavern without a sunstone anywhere in sight. That spark of his was frustrating. Why'd it have to be wasted on someone like him?

What was more, I *wanted* to show him up. He'd done nothing but antagonize me from the moment we'd met, and someone needed to put him in his place. It's just…well, I wasn't good enough to do it.

Lilia patted me on the bum, hard enough to launch me through the arched gate. I stumbled forward, and a cloud of dirt billowed around me. The cheering of the crowd dimmed, and I felt the weight of a thousand eyes settle on my face. A face that was flaming like a dragon's breath.

Swallowing, I ignored my pounding heart and

lifted my chin, striding into the center of the arena, where the other competitors waited for me. There were fewer this year than in previous competitions, I noted. Usually, around twenty participated. But other than Tormund and his two pals, only six dwarves stood ready in the circle drawn in the sand. That made ten of us in total.

That bettered my odds.

I shook my head at myself, clenching my teeth. It didn't *better my odds*. What in fate's name was I thinking? I knew all these dwarves. They trained year in and year out for these trials, honing their skills. Most of them even weighed their food to ensure they consumed enough grub to fuel their bodies. I wondered if Tormund did the same...

As I approached the group, his broad, shadow-wreathed form tugged at my gaze. I couldn't help but turn toward him, despite the talking to I'd given myself before coming here. I didn't want to give him the satisfaction of any more attention.

He was looking right at me. A smile curved his lips, and then he winked.

A furious heat flooded my cheeks. Who did he think he was? Honestly, I wished he'd come into my house again just so I could kick him right back out with magic. It would serve him right, waltzing in here with—

"Astrid," a voice said from beside me. I blinked.

Jostein's face materialized just to my right. He was frowning at me, his brow furrowed in concern. "Are you quite all right, my love?"

"Yes, of course," I replied, my throat tight.

"Hmm. You just take it easy, you hear? This first trial is the strength one." He pounded me on the back, then walked over to welcome each of the other contestants. All of them were staring at me like I was a corpse come to life.

When he'd finished, Jostein strode into the center of the arena with his hands outstretched. The lingering cheers died, and a pregnant silence descended on the packed stands.

"Welcome to the Eighteenth Annual Fittest Under the Mountain!" he exclaimed, his white bushy beard bouncing with every word.

The deafening roar of four thousand dwarves pounded against my eardrums. I lifted my gaze to scan the crowd in the circular stands, suddenly feeling as small as a grain of dirt. It looked different, seeing it all from down here. There were so many people eagerly awaiting a demonstration of strength, speed, agility, and endurance. None of which I really had.

My eyes drifted back to Tormund's face as Jostein continued his yearly speech to signify the start of the trials. But for once, I didn't catch Tormund's stare. Head cocked, he was examining

Galinn, who stood tall in the center of the cluster of dwarves, beaming like he'd already won the damn thing.

As if sensing the weight of my eyes, Tormund shifted his gaze my way. He arched a brow and inclined his head toward Galinn. I nodded back.

"Let the first trial begin!" Jostein suddenly exclaimed, interrupting our silent conversation.

I swallowed, dragging my attention back to the task at hand. Jostein motioned toward a row of ten large stones that sat waiting behind a black line drawn in the dirt. At the other end of the arena stretched another line. The beginning and the end.

"Each of you will move a stone to the other side of the arena," Jostein instructed. "Whoever is fastest wins."

It was a simple enough task, especially for those of us who worked in the mines. We moved rocks around all the time, though the carts helped us across longer distances. I eyed the stones. They came up to my knees and looked pretty damn heavy. I usually left ones this size for others to deal with.

Tormund swaggered over and elbowed me in the side. "You still plan on showing me how much I've underestimated you?"

My hands fisted. "I wasn't talking about the competition."

"Oh? You could have fooled me." Chuckling, he moved off—probably to annoy the other contestants. That seemed to be his strategy.

I ground my teeth and scanned the crowd for a familiar flash of silver hair, but the faces were nothing more than a blur. Right now, I sorely needed Lilia's encouraging smile. She'd remind me that Tormund didn't matter. None of this did. She'd tell me to make a game of it, to let go and have a little fun.

But since she wasn't by my side, I had to repeat the words in my head. I had no chance of winning, and that was fine. I'd come last in most—probably all—of these trials. Again, no need to cry about it! I'd move the stone as far as I could, then have a tankard of brew and some moss cakes with my friends. Maybe a bit of my leftover chocolate, too.

It would be a lovely way to spend the evening.

Nodding to myself, I followed the others to the starting position and took a spot behind the stone furthest down the line. Thankfully, Tormund had decided to go to the middle, so I wouldn't have to suffer his taunting jabs when I fell behind.

"But before we begin," Jostein suddenly shouted, "we have a surprise for this year's winner!"

A hush went through the crowd. Two dwarves I didn't recognize strolled through the arched gate balancing a large sculpture beneath a fluttering red cloth. Long gauzy gowns swept down to their sandalled feet, and their hair was twisted into intricate patterns and decorated with blue tinkling bells. The color of their bells meant they were from Rockheim, an enormous city that was a month-long trek south through the mountains.

I straightened as they approached Jostein. Most residents of Rockheim didn't venture this far north, not even for the trials. Too backwoods and boring, I'd often heard them say. And yet they'd come bearing some kind of prize...When they reached Jostein's side, he turned toward me and gave me a meaningful stare. And without further comment, he whisked the cloth off the statue they held.

A gleaming emerald shard erupted with light. I gasped and stumbled back, so caught off guard, my legs nearly twisted beneath me. I'd read its description a hundred thousand times, and yet I still wasn't prepared for how brutally beautiful it was. Life itself seemed to pour from its flickering depths, and the buzz of its power filled my head.

But the sound soon vanished beneath the thunder of four thousand dwarves cheering and clapping and stomping their feet on the ground.

"That's the Everstone," the dwarf beside me exclaimed.

"It damn well is," I said, my heart pounding.

The Everstone was finally here and right in my grasp...but it wasn't mine. After all the *effort* and the hoping and dreaming, I hadn't found it. I'd been looking in the wrong place. It'd been in the southern mines, and I never would have thought to look there. I'd been convinced it was north all this time.

I'd spent all my life chasing something that I'd never been fated to find. And there was only one way I could get it now.

My pulse thrummed in my neck.

Moments stretched by, and the cheers grew louder. I swallowed the lump of sunstone in my throat. Eventually, Jostein lifted his hand, and the thunderous sound died.

"As I'm sure you've all guessed, the champion of this year's games will win the Everstone," he said, his voice more hushed now than before. "This stone holds great power. Whoever wins these trials will have earned it."

I leaned forward to look down the row of contestants. Tormund stood with his head cocked, a furrow on his brow that likely matched my own troubled expression. Hmm. That was odd. I'd assumed he'd be thrilled by this development. He wanted to win the trials, and he wanted the damn stone. This way, he could kill two birds with... well, *one stone.*

I would have laughed at my own joke, but the thickening disappointment in my gut held it back.

"Can you believe this?" Knut asked from beside me, eagerly rubbing his hands together. "This year is going to be *my* year, I can feel it."

I frowned. "What makes you think you can beat Galinn?" Or Tormund, for that matter. Because as grudging as I was to accept it, there was something about the shadow demon that told me he'd do well in all these tasks. Perhaps he wouldn't have the greatest strength in the field, but he was quick on his feet, he was smarter than I'd given him credit for, and he was determined. Mental toughness went a long way in games like this.

Knut scoffed. "Galinn has won far too many times. He's past his prime, and I've come close in the past."

Knut had in fact not come close. He'd come second, but there'd been miles between him and Galinn every time. And it would continue that way for a while.

Dwarves lived long, long lives. Not as long as elves, but much longer than humans. It was useful when working in the mines. Those of us who took up the pickaxe had years to craft our expertise and efficiency, honing our skills to perfection. Our prime lasted decades. Galinn was still a young lad, especially compared to some of the other contestants in the arena. He likely wouldn't hit his peak for another ten years, if not more.

"I think he still has some fight left in him," I said gently.

But Knut rubbed his hands together, shaking his head to dismiss my words. "No, he's had his time. Someone needs to make a comeback, especially with the Everstone up for grabs. That makes for a much better story, don't you think?"

I loosed a bitter laugh. "If it's a good story that you're after, then I'm the one who should win."

He cocked his head and studied me. "You know what? You're right. Fates, I'd love it if you snatched the win from Galinn's greedy paws."

I raised my brow. "It was a joke, Knut."

"But what an amazing joke it would be to see the look on Galinn's face when *you*, of all dwarves, took the win from him after he's dominated for so bloody long. To get the Everstone. What a story, Astrid. If only you had the skills to do it."

Heaving a sigh, I turned my attention back onto the Everstone, gleaming in the distance. "I'm getting really tired of everyone thinking I suck."

"Then prove us all wrong."

My hands curled by my sides, almost into fists. A part of me deep down wanted to do just that. I could picture it all in my mind's eye. Me, sprinting across the finish line first. Me, raising my hands before the cheering crowd. Me, clutching the Ever-stone to my chest and making my wish. Asking it for the freedom to explore the lands beyond these mountainous walls.

My prison cell.

My caged bars.

My invisible bonds that trapped me in place.

I'd never done anything to deserve my curse. It was high time I broke free.

But all those thoughts quickly deflated. I had the worst odds of anyone out here. Astrid Balstad would not be winning any trials, let alone enough of them to get the Everstone. I'd have to watch someone else take it, along with any hope of seeing the glorious sunrise over the mountain peaks.

6

ASTRID

Jostein held up his hands, quieting the roaring crowd. The hush that followed was somehow louder than the cheers.

"Now that you know what's at stake, we shall begin," Jostein intoned, looking at each contestant in turn, his eyes alight with excitement. "I hope to see some good efforts today. Stand beside your stones and prepare yourselves. When the dwarven bell tolls, race your bloody hearts out."

Pulling a deep breath into my lungs, I bent my knees and placed my trembling hands on my stone. All around me, the other contestants did the same. A long stretch of silence followed, tension building like a powerful drumbeat. And then the bell tolled.

An explosion of grunts followed as the contestants heaved the rocks into their arms and began stumbling across the sandy ground. I, on the other hand, took a different approach. I'd already determined there was no way in fate's name I could carry the damn thing. Instead, I clenched my teeth and shoved it a little. Might as well appear as if I were trying, at least until the others crossed the finish line.

The rock inched forward in a slight roll.

My breath puffed from my lungs, and I shoved again. Once more, the rock rolled a little closer to the finish line. Not that *close* was a good descriptor. I was still yards away.

I pushed again. And again. My arms ached from the effort, though I was using the strength in my legs to do most of the work. After a good ten rolls, sweat glistened on my brow, and I glanced up to see I'd made it a quarter of the way across the arena.

Huh.

Many of the other contestants were already halfway by now, but a few were behind me, surprisingly enough. Galinn and Tormund were only steps from the finish line, neck and neck. The crowd's cheers were thunderous. Everyone was on their feet, stomping and screaming and waving banners in the air, the colors signifying who they supported. I was green and gold. To my surprise, I spotted a few here and there.

I shoved the stone again with a bit more effort than before. It rolled forward, tumbling at least five feet ahead of me. Eyes widening, I glanced at the floor, noticing the almost imperceptible slope toward the finish line. My heart pounded, but I forced my face to remain as defeated as before. Hopefully, no one behind me had noticed the slope. So far, I was the only one rolling the stone. Pride kept the others from doing anything other than hauling the damn thing around and straining beneath all that weight.

As nonchalantly as possible, I palmed the rock and shoved it again, releasing a loud groan to make it seem like I was struggling.

The stone tumbled forward. Smiling, I shoved it again, and it kept rolling forward, gaining momentum with every push.

I passed Knut on my left. He whooped and hollered, urging me on.

The crowd roared with thunderous approval. I glanced around the stone, expecting to see Tormund or Galinn rushing to victory, but…no, they'd already finished. They stood behind the black line and lounged against their rocks, and they were watching—me.

Tormund locked eyes with me and smiled.

My gut twisted. Cheeks heating, I shoved the rock again, catching up to one of Tormund's shadow demon friends. The crowd's cheers had grown deafening. I couldn't even hear myself breathe, let alone think. Sweat drenching the back of my neck and hands aching from scraping the rock, I ground my teeth and gave the stone one last push.

It tipped over, and over, and over again, shuddering to a stop just behind the finish line. I jogged after it. My feet passed over the line. The crowd went wild.

I bit back a smile, but then I couldn't help my damn self. My lips widened, a strange surge of pride lifting my chest. Grinning, I looked up and scanned the arena stands. Everyone was on their feet. Green and gold banners whipped through the air. And even though there were nine other contestants, and even though I hadn't won—five others had finished before me—I knew deep in my gut that all this screaming...it was for me.

Little old me.

Tormund sauntered over and stuck out his hand. "Well done, Astrid."

The light in my heart suddenly died. I ignored his offered hand. "Don't patronize me, Tormund. I'm assuming you won?"

"I did." A pause. "But I mean what I said. Well

done on your finish. Lots of the dwarves bet you'd come last. Looks like I was right, and they were wrong."

"You were right—wait what?" I asked, stumbling over my words.

"I bet you'd come middle of the pack," he said, smiling now. "You just made me a lot of gold coin."

He looked at me like he expected some kind of thanks, like I should be grateful he'd believed in me—as half-hearted as it was. He'd bet on me? For the middle of the pack? Who did he think he was? My scowl deepened. He thought he was the bloomin' winner of the first trial, that was who. And to make matters more annoying, he'd succeeded in his egotistical mission.

At least he didn't think I'd fail miserably, like everyone else.

Pressing my lips together, I shoved that thought aside.

"Congratulations," I said tightly.

He laughed. "Your nose does this funny little scrunching thing when you're annoyed. It's kind of cute. Want a cut of my winnings for betting on you?"

"No, I do not want a cut of your winnings," I said, throwing up my hands in exasperation and very pointedly ignoring his comment about my nose. "I want you to leave me out of your games."

He leaned in close, and his lips brushed my ear. A shiver unexpectedly coursed through my body. "Just take your win for what it is, love. The only person you need to beat is your past self, and you did that in spades. Because the girl I met yesterday never would have come sixth. In fact, I don't think she would have even tried."

I bristled, narrowing my eyes. Through gritted teeth, I said, "That's rich coming from you. You wouldn't be happy coming sixth."

"I need the Everstone. I know you think you do, too. But you don't. Not really."

"Don't you dare tell me what I do and don't need." My voice echoed through the cavernous space. It was then I realized the crowd had quieted. It was so silent in the arena now that you could hear a sunstone drop. Or—much to my intense embarrassment—Tormund and I arguing about which one of us deserved the Everstone more.

Tormund leaned back, a hiss escaping through clenched teeth, as if he'd noticed the silence at the same moment I had. His eyes met mine, and for a moment, he felt like the only person in this gods-forsaken mountain who understood everything I was feeling. The embarrassment, yes. But also the defiance against anyone who might laugh at said embarrassment. And the slight hope that the other contestants might get rattled by our combined stubbornness.

But there was something else I noticed. That spark brightened his eyes again as his lips twisted into a grin. I couldn't stop myself from grinning right back. The *entire* arena was watching us, collective breath held as they waited to see what we'd do next.

So, with that in mind, I stuck out my hand. "To putting on a good show."

A chuckle rumbled from his chest. "To entertaining the bloody lot of them."

His fingers tightened around mine. Warmth flooded my skin, despite the cooling shadows that twisted around his body. I swallowed, jumping when the roar of the crowd engulfed us once again. We shook hands. Tormund nodded once, his eyes locked on mine.

I nodded back, though I didn't know what for. I just felt compelled to do it, like something in his gaze had tugged my chin up and then down again. It was why, a moment later, I still held his hand. Because his alluring shadow demon gaze was controlling me. Not for any other reason. Especially not because the warmth of him called to me.

Sucking in a sharp breath, I yanked back my hand and took a step away.

I stumbled right into Galinn's chest and winced

from the hardness of it. Galinn grabbed my arms and pushed me sideways. My feet twisted on the sloped ground. I threw out my hands to catch my fall, but my knees hit the sandy dirt first. Pain lanced through me, as viciously sharp as a knife.

"You cheated," Galinn said, pointing a finger at Tormund's chest.

Ignoring Galinn, Tormund knelt beside me and held out a hand. "You all right?"

I rubbed my knees. "Yes, yes, I'm fine."

Narrowing his eyes, Tormund glared up at Galinn. "You knocked over another contestant. Surely that gets you disqualified."

A deep angry red spread through Galinn's face, but then he looked at me and regret filled his eyes. He rubbed the back of his neck, frowning. "I'm sorry, Astrid. I only meant to move you out of the way."

Jostein bustled over to us, twisting his hands around his beard. "You three are causing quite the commotion." He looked down at where I still sat on the ground. "Astrid, tell me you're fine."

"I'm fine, Jostein. Don't worry, I—"

"Galinn knocked her onto the ground. She seems fine, but he could have really hurt her. I thought that kind of behavior wasn't tolerated." Tormund stood, though he still kept his hand stretched out to me. "I read the rules before entering. No sabotaging other contestants, no outright hostility, and certainly no bodily harm."

Jostein pursed his lips.

"You can't honestly be listening to this *stranger*," Galinn argued, the red in his face deepening. "He doesn't even belong in this competition in the first place. And he cheated!"

"I did not cheat," Tormund countered.

"You used your shadow demon power."

"No one said I couldn't."

I heaved a sigh, rolling my eyes. This was getting ridiculous now.

"He's right," Jostein cut in, stepping between them. "Accident or no, you very clearly shoved Astrid hard enough to make her fall. I'm afraid I have to disqualify you from the competition. That includes all future ones, too."

As if the God of Thunder were listening to Jostein's words, the metal fist pendant vanished from Galinn's tunic. Dumbstruck, he stood there, his mouth hanging open. I felt a little dumbstruck myself. Jostein had never disqualified someone before, and certainly not the winner for five years in a row.

Suddenly, the competition was wide open. I glanced over at Tormund. His smug smile told me everything I needed to know.

Eventually, Galinn wandered off and Jostein

declared Tormund the winner of the first trial. The applause was more muted than before. There were likely a great deal of people who'd bet a lot of gold on Galinn's win, and they'd already lost it all. I didn't move from my spot on the ground, too busy watching the whole thing play out. No one was paying much attention to me anymore.

When the spectators finally began to leave the stands, Tormund ventured back over and stuck out his hand again. "Would you like some help, or are you going to stay there for the rest of the evening?"

I pushed myself to my feet, ignoring his hand. "I know what you did there."

He arched a brow. "Whatever do you mean?"

"You weren't concerned about me, and you don't really care about the rules. But you'd take any opportunity to get rid of the contestant most likely to win."

"I'm the contestant most likely to win," he countered.

"You certainly are now."

Tormund shrugged. "And so what if I saw an opportunity and jumped on it? Do you blame me?"

"You pretended you were concerned for me, so yes. I don't like liars who use others for their own gain."

"You're just annoyed I'm going to win the Everstone. I have need for it, you know."

I folded my arms. "What need?"

He glanced around. There were still several contestants nearby and hundreds of spectators milling around the stands. Dropping his voice to a low murmur, he said, "Not here. Too many people. Come to my camp tonight, and I'll tell you everything you want to know about Tormund Bakke."

"Tempting, but I'm not sure I want to converse with someone who refers to himself in the third person."

"I have cake," he offered.

I squinted at him. "All right. Maybe I'll come. But only because I want to know your reason. And I won't stay long."

"You'll find me in the cavern camp near The Wet Beard. See you tonight, Astrid."

7

TORMUND

"What do you mean you asked her to come here?" Altan deposited another log on the fire in the center of our circle of tents. Dwarves didn't seem to rely on fires for warmth. Their sunstones emitted heat and even helped them grow their crops. But it didn't feel right to spend an evening without flames, so we'd brought enough logs with us to last a week.

Meral sat hunched on the ground, whittling a plank of wood she'd brought with her. Half was already carved into the shape of a horse's head. It would only take her another day to sort the second half out. I'd never met anyone who was a better woodcarver. Reis, Altan's partner and our assistant for the games, was off doing who knew what—

likely drinking the night away at The Wet Beard, shouting the words to the dwarven folk songs he'd already memorized.

"I think Astrid and I got off on the wrong foot. I thought if I tell her why I need the Everstone, she won't be so prickly toward me," I said.

"Who cares if she's prickly? We didn't come here to make friends," Meral said, glancing up, her shadows whipping around her face and hands.

"And maybe she's just a prickly person," Altan added.

"I doubt that. Besides, she's the expert on the Everstone. I need her to not hate me," I said.

Meral waved her wooden piece in the air. "Bah. You can win it through the competition now. You don't need Astrid's knowledge anymore."

"Except I don't know how to actually *use* the Everstone's power after I win it."

Altan knelt beside the logs and stoked the fire with a long metal stick. "How hard can it be? Just ask it for what you want, and I'm sure it'll give it to you."

But that seemed too easy. In fact, all of it seemed too easy. Ever since I'd laid eyes on the Everstone back in the arena, my stomach had tangled into knots. There it was, the elusive gem that held the power I'd coveted for so many years. All I had to do was win the dwarven competition, something I'd already planned to do. And it would be mine.

No hunting the mines. No following Astrid during her daily tasks. No coaxing out information with encouraging smiles and witty banter that made her face light up and that tinkling laugh fall from her lips. Fates, that laugh was a gorgeous thing.

But nevermind that. I couldn't shake the feeling that something wasn't quite right…

"Surprised you put your tent here instead of outside my cottage so you could spy on me all day and night," called out Astrid, her lilting voice almost singing to the tune of the bells jingling in her hair.

She stepped into the cave and looked around. A few other strangers to the mountain—spectators from the other Isles—had packed into the space as well. There were about a hundred of us in total, building fires, cooking food, and sharing whatever supplies we'd brought with us. Some had even hung their banners on their tents to signify who they supported this year. It made it all feel a bit festive.

I slung my hands into my trouser pockets and crossed the distance between us. "What an excellent idea. Would you like to help me move my tent?"

She laughed, her eyes crinkling in the corners. My chest lifted.

"Guess there's no need for that anymore, eh? The bloomin' gem's been found."

"Yes," I said, frowning. "About that."

She squinted at me. "You've got that look on your face again. The same expression you had when Jostein revealed the Everstone. I thought you'd be thrilled Rockheim found it."

"It's a lovely coincidence," I said. "Like the gods themselves lined things up just for me."

Or you.

I didn't want to alarm Astrid, but some of my unease was very much originating from her direction. She had not entered the competition herself. At first, I'd thought little of it. Anyone could have put forth her name. Someone might believe in her more than she believed in herself and thought she was worthy of a win. Or maybe someone was playing a prank. They thought it would be funny to see her flail around. Why? Maybe she'd annoyed the wrong person years ago, and they were just now getting their revenge.

But then the Everstone had appeared. Everyone knew Astrid was desperate for the stone. I'd already heard dozens of dwarves talking about it. And it just so happened to be the champion's prize the same year she'd been entered against her will. What were the bloody odds of that?

She scrunched her cute little nose. "Now that you say it like that, it does sound strange. The same year you enter is the same year that the champion's prize is the stone."

Gods, she could have taken the words right out of my head. Only she was talking about me, and I was talking about her.

"Unnerving, right?"

"Very." She frowned. "What do you make of it?"

"I'm not sure yet." I turned and gestured toward the circle of tents. Altan and Meral had made themselves scarce, though I had a feeling they were lurking close enough to eavesdrop on every word Astrid and I exchanged.

Nosy bastards.

Astrid followed me to the campfire and plopped down on the log Altan had been using as a chair. She held out her hands, warming herself on the fire. The flames cast an orange glow across her face that matched the gorgeous shade of her hair.

I blinked and cleared my throat. "I'm surprised you came."

She shrugged. "You said you had cake."

"Oh, that's right." Chuckling, I pulled the wrapped cake from my pack and tossed it her way. She caught it one-handed and had it unwrapped before I'd managed to take a seat. Her eyes widened at the creamy frosting and the rich crimson cake.

"Bloomin' fates. What is *this*?" she breathed.

"Red Demon Cake with buttermilk frosting. Try it. You'll love it."

She bit into the cake without hesitation, frosting coating her upper lip. Her eyes rolled back into her head, and she moaned. "This is amazing. You have to give me the recipe."

"Gladly," I said. "Though you won't find most of the ingredients under the mountain."

Her face fell. She wiped the frosting off her lip. "Of course not."

"Sorry. You could still make it, but it'll require a trip above ground to trade with the sailors or the other Isles," I said.

She cleared her throat. "You said you were going to tell me why you want the Everstone."

"And I will." I leaned forward, my elbows resting on my knees. "But I'm going to need something for you in return."

"I see. That's why you're buttering me up with cake."

"And is it working?"

"Depends on what you want."

"Tell me where you thought you'd find the Everstone."

A tense silence followed. Astrid took another bite of the cake and chewed thoughtfully before she swallowed hard and said, "I'll tell you that, but I need something from *you* in return." She shot me a wolfish smile.

"Ha! All right. What's your request?"

"I want to know why you're asking me this question."

I studied her carefully. Astrid studied me right back. It was as if we were dancing around a conversation we both wanted to have but didn't quite trust the other enough to voice. At the end of the day, I didn't know this lass, and she was a competitor. She'd do whatever it took to get her hands on the Everstone—she was cursed, after all—even if that meant betraying my confidence.

Because what would there be to betray? We were strangers.

And yet I found myself saying, "It's like I said earlier, something doesn't feel right about that gem."

"And you want to know where I thought I'd find it. As in, you want to know if I thought it'd be in Rockheim? Which means you're not sure it would have been." She leaned forward. "You don't think it's a fake, do you?"

"It certainly didn't look or feel like a fake."

As soon as the dwarves had unveiled the Everstone, a rippling power had washed across my skin. Whatever that thing was, it wasn't devoid of magic. It did *something*. I just wasn't convinced it did what we all thought.

She nibbled on her bottom lip. "There's a tunnel not far from The Wet Beard. For a really long time, I was convinced it was there, but I've explored every inch of it multiple times. It's not there."

I arched my brow. "I think I'd like to see that tunnel."

"And I don't think I'm keen to show it to you."

"I've got more of that cake," I said, pointing at the red crumbs scattered around her boots.

"Using my weaknesses against me is extremely unfair." She stuck out her hand, palm up. "Gimme."

"Gladly." I passed her the cake, but instead of digging in straight away, she tucked it into the leather satchel slung around her shoulders. "But first, tell me why you want the Everstone."

I sighed. I *had* agreed to do just that, but it wasn't something I much liked speaking of, least of all to someone I barely knew. But I couldn't back out now. If I did, she'd never help me. I'd just keep it short and sweet.

"My brother is ill. The Everstone has enough power to heal him."

She sat a little straighter on the log. "Ill? I'm sorry. What's his affliction?"

"It's some kind of skin issue," I said tightly. "It means he cannot withstand the sun's rays. He's destined to remain in the darkness unless I find him a cure."

Astrid blinked at me. Her lips pressed together into a harsh white line. And there was so much forced pity in her expression that it made me wish I could take back my words. She likely thought what everyone else did: why would a shadow demon even care? We loved the dark. But Tahir yearned for the sun's rays, and he needed the world above. I'd do anything to give it to him.

"That must be difficult for him," Astrid eventually said.

"No need to be sarcastic." I rose. It was time to end this conversation and explore the tunnel Astrid had mentioned.

She stood, brushing the crumbs from her shirt. "I'm not being sarcastic. I feel for the lad and wouldn't wish that fate on anyone."

"Most people point out that shadow demons thrive in the darkness," I said slowly.

"No one should have to remain in the darkness forever, not even a shadow demon."

Something in my chest stirred. I cleared my throat, at a loss for words. Not something I often experienced. A moment ago, the last thing I'd wanted to do was confide in Astrid. She clearly hated me. And I wasn't too fond of her, either.

But she'd listened to my story—the little of it I'd told—and she'd *heard* me.

That didn't mean I'd let her have the Everstone, though. It was mine.

8

ASTRID

I led the way past The Wet Beard, my heartbeat pounding in time with my heavy steps. The tavern was heaving this time of night. Dwarves were packed inside. Some leapt on top of tables, stomping their feet as they slurred the words of the bard's latest tune. Several elves, pixies, and humans had joined them—spectators who had travelled from the other Isles. Many of them were likely sharing the cavern camp with Tormund and his friends, but they'd chosen the tavern and its festive atmosphere to pass the evening. The dwarves would celebrate long into the night.

My brow furrowed as I ruminated on Tormund's confession. His brother's affliction sounded a lot like my own, though mine was a curse and his was an illness. Still, what were the bloomin' odds? And how did a shadow demon come down with something like that? They thrived in the shadows, fed upon them. I had to admit, Tormund's powers were likely why he had done so well in the first trial.

These trials had been designed with dwarves in mind, but the darkness of The Deep was perfect for shadow demons.

Lost in thought, I nearly missed the tunnel's entrance. I came to a sudden stop at the mouth of the mine. Tormund ran into me. Breath knocked from my lungs, I stumbled forward, but his hand caught me before I fell again.

The heat of his palm seeped into my skin. Gods, he was so bloomin' warm.

"That would have been the third time my presence made you faint," he said, though his voice still held traces of the tension from earlier. He'd practically had to force out his story about his brother, what little he'd said. I'd wanted to know more—so much more—but it was clearly difficult for him to talk about, so I hadn't pushed.

"What did I tell you about egos and tunnels?" I asked, turning to face him. He hovered right there, only an inch away. I swallowed hard and backed up.

"Even a dragon-sized ego could fit inside this

one." He gestured down the tunnel, still lit by the sunstones scattered around the floor. A mine cart sat just inside the entrance, overflowing with the gems. Soon, someone would come along to take them to the homes or bridges that needed them.

"You haven't seen the end of it yet," I replied crisply.

We started down the tunnel. As Tormund had noticed, it started plenty wide enough for us to walk side by side. Now and then, Tormund commented on what he saw. The first mining station held pickaxes of every size. He asked if we should grab some. I firmly told him no. Then he noticed the green mineral veins forking through the stone walls. He pointed out that they were the same color as the Everstone.

"Very good," I said. "I wondered how long it would take you to notice that."

"That's why you thought it was down here. Because of the mineral traces."

"Seems like the logical conclusion," I said with a shrug.

He eyed me as we passed another cluster of sunstones jutting from the carved stone wall. "There's more you're not saying."

I ground my teeth. How was he so good at reading me? We'd known each other for all of a day, and I wasn't sure *know* was the right word for whatever this was. Acquainted? Still didn't feel right. We were like two ships passing in the night. Not that I'd ever seen a damn ship in my life, other than in the books that passed through now and again. Leather-bound tomes were another thing that was too fragile for the humidity in The Deep. We had a library above ground, of course, but I hated asking others to grab the books for me.

"I don't know what gives you that impression," I snapped.

"You're tense."

"Yes, you seem to cause that reaction in me."

He shot me a wolfish smile. "It's my muscly charm, isn't it?"

I rolled my eyes. "I never should have mentioned your bloomin' muscles."

"You're right. You shouldn't have." Slinging his hands into his pockets, he sauntered beside me in that ridiculous swagger of his. "Because now I will never let you forget it."

"Luckily, you'll be long gone in a fortnight, and I'll never have to hear about it again," I replied with a sweet smile.

"Until next year. When I come back to compete again." He waggled his brow at me.

I slowed to a stop. "Surely not."

"Why not? I could be the new Galinn the Great

and win five years in a row. Or six, actually. I'd have to beat his record, of course. It would make me the longest-running champion of your dwarven games."

Narrowing my eyes, I continued down the tunnel at a brisk pace. I needed to get this done and dusted, so I could go home to my plants. Tormund easily kept up with me, his strides long and purposeful. Bloomin' shadow demons and their bloomin' long legs.

After a moment of silence, he asked, "Aren't you going to make a cutting remark about my ego?"

"Not necessary," I replied. "The next trial will put you in your place without me having to say a word."

"What's the next task?"

I stopped again, sighing heavily. "You don't even know?"

"Why would I? I've never been Under the Mountain before."

"Because, I don't know, you'd done some kind of preparation before you came here?" I threw up my hands. "Most strangers who enter usually do. It never really helps, mind you, but at least they have the decency to try. You…you just think you can show up here completely unprepared and win the whole bloomin' thing without trying!"

He took a step closer to me, grinning wickedly. "You're doing that nose-scrunching thing again."

I tensed, then rubbed my nose. "Stop it."

"Stop what? Making your nose scrunch?" Then, much to my horror, he tapped said nose. "Why in fate's name would I do that? It's so cute when you do it."

Heat bloomed in my cheeks. Scrunching my nose—gods, I really was doing it, I realized—I turned away and pointed emphatically at the tunnel walls. "Fine. You're right. There's more I'm not saying. Notice anything about the sunstones?"

We'd only walked several yards around the bend. The distant sound of singing dwarves still reached our ears, and the tunnel had yet to narrow. And yet there were sunstones everywhere. Curious to see if his mind worked fast enough, I cocked my head and watched him stare at the gems.

After a moment, he glanced back at the bend, then looked at the gems again, noting the over-flowing carts here and there. "How long's The Wet Beard been in business?"

"Decades," I replied.

He nodded. "Just like the trading shops, I presume?"

"That's right."

"This tunnel is heavily used. It has been for a while. And yet there are hundreds of sunstones still embedded in these walls. We're barely down the tunnel. Shouldn't you have mined them all by now?"

"You'd think," I said, impressed he'd gotten it so quickly. "They grow back. And this is the only place Under the Mountain where they do that."

"That plus these mineral traces…" He rubbed the base of his curving horns, brow furrowed. "Well, that's that, then. We need to search this tunnel for the Everstone. The other must be a fake."

I took a step back in the direction of The Wet Beard. "I hate to be the bearer of bad news, but you're wrong, Tormund. I've spent my entire life looking for that stone. In this very tunnel. I followed the mineral traces. I dug my pickaxe into the densest clusters of sunstones. It's not here. It never was. The miners of Rockheim found it instead."

He stared at me for a long moment, his expression unreadable. "Surely you don't believe that."

I wasn't sure what I believed. I'd seen the Everstone with my own two eyes, but more importantly, I'd felt its power. There was no faking that. Besides, what would Rockheim have to gain by tricking everyone into believing the stone was up for grabs? It made little sense.

Still, something about the whole thing didn't sit right with me, either…

And if Tormund *was* right and the Everstone was still in these tunnels, I couldn't very well help him find it.

So I said, "I'd *like* to think it's here. Mostly because I'm not going to win the trials, now am I? But it's time to accept reality and move on. Didn't you feel the power of the gem they showed us? If it was a fake, it wouldn't have any magic."

"Sunstones have magic," he countered.

"Not like that," I said. "I'm telling you, this is all a coincidence and nothing more. The Everstone was never here."

"Hmm." He rubbed his chin, frowning down the tunnel. For a moment, it looked like he might listen to me. I started to turn back toward the mouth of the tunnel, already looking forward to a moss cake, a cup of tea, and a whole lot of bloomin' quiet. My ears were still ringing from the stomping and the cheering in the arena, and all I wanted now was the company of my plants.

But then Tormund started walking in the opposite direction of The Wet Beard.

"Where are you going?" I propped fisted hands on my hips.

Without even slowing, he tossed the words over his shoulder. "I'm going to take a look myself."

I let out a little growl and strode after him.

"Come on," I said, practically running to catch

up. "It's late, and I'm tired, and I've already searched these tunnels five million times."

"Then go on home," he practically sang. "I think I can manage on my own from now on."

"Absolutely bloomin' not."

He kept walking. "You worried I'll find something?"

"No."

Yes, actually. He seemed destined to have every little thing fall right into his lap. I never should have brought him here. If that other Everstone was a fake, I had very little doubt Tormund would find the real one if he put even a flicker of effort into it.

As he moved around the next bend, I grabbed his arm. He tensed against my fingers, but he came to a stop. His eyes dropped to meet mine, his shadows whorling around him, bigger and quicker now that we were leaving the sunstone-laden section behind.

He arched a single brow, those midnight eyes burrowing into me. "Yes, Astrid?"

There was something about the way he said my name…

I cleared my throat and dropped my hand. "You shouldn't go further, at least not alone."

"And why ever not?"

"It's dangerous."

"I'm a shadow demon. I know how to move

around in the dark," he said, his voice near a purr now.

"Maybe so, but not in mines. It's different here than in your caves back home."

"And you've visited Azraak, have you?" His eyes dipped to my chest, and when he dragged them back up to my face, there was a different sort of spark there. And that was when I remembered other stories I'd been told. Shadow demons fed upon darkness. It made them powerful and strong, but also something *else*.

"No," I breathed. "I've never visited your homeland, but I know you don't mine there. You don't need sunstones."

"Ah, but we do need gold." He took a step closer to me. I backed up and hit the slick stone wall. "And there are caverns near Azraak full of it."

"Wait…so you mine? None of the other shadow demons have ever mentioned it."

He winked. "Only a few of us know where the gold caverns are. And we don't like to share."

Suddenly, his overbearing confidence made a lot more sense. If Tormund was a miner, of course he'd come prepared. He likely spent every day working the pickaxe, hauling rocks, and even scaling ropes. And everyone here was none the wiser.

"I still don't think you should go further alone,"

I said. "Just because you mine for gold doesn't mean you know anything about dwarven tunnels."

"You're welcome to come along." He smiled and motioned toward the distant, raucous singing. "Or you can relax, put up your feet, and have an ale. Up to you."

"I was going to have a cup of tea, thanks, but that's not what I meant. It's time for you to return to camp, Tormund."

"No, thank you," he said, then took off down the tunnel again.

I fisted my hands and groaned.

"That little growl is almost as cute as your nose scrunch. Almost," he called out. "Now you go have a good night. I'll tell you tomorrow if I find the Everstone."

"You're bloomin' mad if you think I'm going to let you do that." And then I took off after him, following the shadow demon into the darkness.

9

ASTRID

"You're right. This is different from our mines in Azraak. Mind telling me why you thought it was a good idea to build a mine track over a chasm? Without any supportive structure?"

I frowned at said mine track. We were deep within the tunnels now, having lost the echo of dwarven song several caves back. So we'd made it to the Bifrost Crossing—named after the ancient bridge to the gods. The ledge on the other side held the entrance to a lower network of tunnels packed tight with sunstones, onyx, and emeralds. We didn't venture that far down unless the tunnels near The Wet Beard ran dry, and that rarely happened. The crossing was difficult to navigate.

Still, it had never been treacherous, like it was now.

Where there had once been a wooden bridge connecting this ledge to the next, now it was nothing but open air. The mine tracks over it had been left behind, so it was just metal railings curving over the darkness.

"The wood must have rotted and collapsed into the chasm," I said, my hollow voice echoing in the cavernous space.

"Hmm. And that usually happens Under the Mountain, does it?" Tormund asked, his voice dripping with skepticism.

"It's very humid down here if you haven't noticed."

"All the other bridges seem fine."

"Most are made from stone," I pointed out. "And stone doesn't rot."

"Interesting. This mine cart here seems just fine." And then he grabbed the wooden side of the cart and leapt inside. It rattled and shook beneath him, the wheels scraping against the iron rails. The thing rolled forward—just an inch—but it was enough to make my heart lurch into my throat.

"Are you mad?" I grabbed the side of the cart, dug in my heels, and held it still. Once those things got going, they *really* got going. Quickly, I jammed the brake into place. "You'll go flying across the chasm if you aren't careful."

"That was the idea," he replied.

"No." I tightened my grip on the cart, shaking my head so emphatically that my jangling bells echoed like an eerie song in the shadowy darkness of the chasm. "We are staying on this side of the chasm, thank you very much."

He levelled his gaze at me. "Don't tell me something as dull as fear can stop you from finding the one thing in this fate-forsaken mountains that could break your curse."

I narrowed my eyes. "Rude."

"Which part?"

"All of it." And despite every instinct telling me not to do it, I hauled myself over the lip of the cart and tumbled right into Tormund's lap, my legs sticking up in the air. Mouth against his thigh, heat blazed through me. I murmured against his trouser's rough fabric, "I didn't think this through."

He laughed—a great booming sound that rumbled through me like the familiar roar of the tavern after a long day toiling away in the mines. I'd never heard him laugh like that until now. All his other chuckles seemed diminished compared to this, like he'd been putting on a show.

"That definitely counts as the third," he said.

"Yes, yes, the third time I've fallen over in your presence," I said, my face still smashed against his leg. I tried not to think about how close my mouth was to *other* parts of him, but it was next to impossible.

"At least you're not denying it anymore." He wrapped firm hands around my waist, easily lifted me into the air, and plopped me right back down—still on his lap. At least this time I was sitting the right way up. My backside was on his legs, and my head was very much sticking up out of the cart, facing forward. In the direction of the chasm.

The deep dark of it loomed before me like the jaws of a hungry beast.

"This is a terrible idea," I muttered under my breath.

"Personally, I'm having a great time," Tormund said. "Now, how do we get this thing going?"

I dropped my head into my palm. There was no backing out now. If I walked away from the situation, Tormund would continue onward without me. And I couldn't let him do that.

Heaving a sigh, I said, "I thought you were a miner. Reach down and pull the brake lever."

"Our set-up isn't as elaborate as yours. We don't have carts and tracks and hundreds of stations set up through the mountain. People would figure out what we were doing if we had too much gear."

I couldn't help but look over my shoulder. "How do you mine without it?"

"Carefully," he replied, as if that answered my question.

Hint: it did not.

But before he could clarify, Tormund swung his arm over the side of the cart, yanked on the brake lever, and then threw his weight forward, careful not to slam into me.

The cart rolled.

I swallowed hard as the world fell out from beneath me. We surged forward so suddenly that my stomach shot up into my throat. All my hair bells rang in warning, and my eyes filled with burning tears. Tormund grabbed my waist and held me against him. The heat of his skin pressed into me, momentarily distracting me from the fact we were rushing over the chasm. Darkness widened its jaws.

A shriek exploded from my throat.

I snatched the side of the cart and held on with all my might. The chasm whirred by, then vanished behind us as we zoomed into the next tunnel. Sunstones flared to life, emitting glowing rays of orange and yellow, filling the tunnel with so much light it was almost blinding.

The cart careened sideways, then slammed into a wall.

We teetered sideways and spilled onto the hard ground. An *"Ergh!"* shot from the depths of me. Bright spots danced in my eyes. Tormund's hand found my waist again. I rolled over, blinking up at him. His concerned face stared back at me. Gone was that ever-present swaggering spark.

"You all right, Astrid?" He brushed a curly strand of ginger hair out of my eyes, his fingers lingering against my skin.

That bloomin' way he said my voice...I shuddered.

His frown deepened. "Astrid? Blink your eyes if you're in pain."

"I'm in pain," I said, pushing up onto my elbows. "But I'm fine."

"You took quite the tumble," he said, gently helping me to my feet.

His careful concern unnerved me. And so I said, "For the fourth time."

Tormund cracked a smile. "For your sake, I hope none of the trials require remaining upright for longer than ten minutes."

I flushed. "Laugh all you want. Your plan has gone sideways. Quite literally."

Tormund looked around the cave we'd entered. It was at the end of a short stretch of tunnel, empty save for the cart and a pair of rails curving into the darkness ahead. We should have carried on with them, but there was a missing section in the track. Melted iron coated the ground, like someone had taken a torch to it.

"I'm starting to think someone doesn't want us poking around down here," Tormund murmured, kneeling beside the melted tracks.

A prickle caressed the back of my neck, and an overwhelming sensation of *wrong* settled over me like smoke so thick I could barely breathe through it. Before, I hadn't truly wanted to believe it—that Tormund was right in his suspicions. Even though I would never win the prize, I didn't like the idea that some dwarves among us were parading around with a fake.

My mountain, nestled in the ridges of The Glass Peaks, was located on the Shard, one of the lands within the Isles of Fable. We had always prided ourselves on being a haven from the rotten things in the world. Greed, violence, destruction, and hate. People were still people, of course, so the Isles weren't perfect. Nowhere was. And here in the dwarven mountains, we took in the prisoners who broke the laws of the Isles.

So we were a little rougher around the edges than some of the other islands.

Still, we'd never had anyone sabotage our mining tracks.

"I'll admit, I'm starting to get that feeling, too," I admitted—rather begrudgingly. Giving Tormund more fuel for believing the Everstone was down here, well…it wasn't my first choice. But we both knew I'd be lying if I said anything else. I nodded toward the tunnel from whence we came. "I'd say we should turn around and go back, but well."

"'But well' is right. I don't much fancy watching you try to balance your way across those rails to the other side of the chasm."

I gave him a blank stare. "I'm really not as clumsy as my recent dexterity seems to suggest."

He motioned toward the chasm. "Then, by all means, have at it."

"No, thank you," I sang. "I will be heading where these tracks lead. There is a larger cave system up ahead, and then the tracks circle back around, coming out four ledges down from The Wet Beard."

Tormund nodded, and we began our journey, walking beside the curve of the tracks. "You know this part of the tunnels, then?"

"Yes, I already told you that. I've spent twenty-six years searching the mines, and that includes this section. All these tunnels connect. I've been through them well over a hundred times."

"Twenty-six years? How young were you when you started?"

"Well, I was five when I started. So I suppose it's been more like nineteen years of searching. But it feels like my whole life. I hardly remember a time before it." I shrugged. "We dwarves start mining young. And as soon as I got a pickaxe in my hand and heard the legend of the Everstone…well, I've been determined to find it ever since."

"I'm only a few years older. And like you, I began my quest at age five." His eyes grew distant. "I didn't know about the Everstone then, of course. I thought I might find answers in my own mountain. I asked every shadow demon in Azraak if they knew of a cure. None did."

I looked up at him. "Then how did you find out about the Everstone?"

"Pure luck," he said. "A year back, I travelled to the mainland when I heard the conquerer Isveig had been removed from his throne. Thought I might help the orcs come out of hiding."

My heart twanged with an unexpected swell of…well, admiration, I supposed. Isveig had been a rotten ruler. He'd stolen the orcish lands, destroyed the dragons, and plotted against the other folk lands. The elves had tried to stop him, but they'd failed.

Eventually, it was his own sister who had defeated him.

Most orcs—the few who'd survived—had gone into hiding. For Tormund to have left his shadowy mountain behind to help them, well. It said a lot about his character.

"Did you see many orcs?" I asked softly.

A wistful smile curled his lips. "More than I even dreamed. The orcs will be all right. I know that now."

"Good. I'd love to see Fafnir one day. I suppose you heard rumors about the Everstone when you were at the docks there?"

He nodded. "Dwarves from Rockheim sailed in to trade. They were talking about it."

"Rockheim, eh?" I tapped my chin, falling into an easy, companionable silence with Tormund as we wound through the tunnels. Now and then, he stopped to examine a cluster of sunstones or another web of mineral lines. But, as it turned out, his luck was no better than mine—at least when it came to this.

Eventually, we reached the rim of the Endless Chasm a few ledges down from The Wet Beard. From the sounds of it, the celebration had turned into a bloomin' riot of good cheer.

"Well." Tormund stuck his hands into his pockets and leaned back on his heels.

"Well," I replied.

"I suppose this is the end of our journey. I'll admit, I believed we'd find the gem in there."

"A part of me thought we would, too, even though I *really have* examined every inch of those tunnels. If it had suddenly appeared, it would have been because someone had put it there."

He rested his back against the wall, his arms crossed over his broad chest. "Strangely, that wouldn't surprise me. Not after everything else that's happened."

"Yeah. Me either." I cleared my throat, eyeing the bridge that would lead me toward my village, my home, and the tea I'd craved a few hours earlier. And then I shifted on my feet, feeling awkward all of a sudden. "So, in case you're turned around, you can take that bridge there to the ledge above. After that, there's another that will take you back to The Wet Beard. You know where to go from there."

"I take it that means you're done with my company for the night," he said in a low murmur.

I swallowed, avoiding his eyes. "If we'd found the Everstone like you'd hoped, what would you have done with it?"

A moment of silence followed, and then he said, "You know what I would have done with it."

My heart sank, but I didn't know why I felt the

suffocating weight of disappointment. He had good reason for wanting that gem, and he'd never pretended he'd let me have it. In fact, he'd been pretty clear that he'd do anything to get his hands on the thing. And yet, something about the decisiveness in his voice stung. He wouldn't even hesitate; he wouldn't consider me at all.

But why would he?

Still, I gazed into his face and searched for any sign that he had empathy for me at all. He wasn't devoid of emotion. He'd proven that by going to see the orcs. So maybe it was just me.

"That's what I thought." I took a step back, my boot scuffing the edge of the bridge. "Have a good night, Tormund."

"Ah, so you're going to hold my love for my brother against me?" He ran his hand along the base of his horns, shaking his head. "Why am I not surprised?"

I furrowed my brow. "Don't act like you know anything about me. You haven't even asked about my *thing*." I couldn't say the word out loud. "For all you know, I could be doomed to die tomorrow."

"Curses never involve death. They're intended to torment the living. The only thing is, Astrid, you seem to be just fine." He cocked his head. "In fact, you have everything you need, and my brother doesn't."

"Except for the one thing I want more than anything," I blurted out.

A beat passed. "The Everstone."

"Yes. No." I threw up my hands. "Nevermind. You wouldn't care about my thing, even if I *could* tell you what it is. Don't ask for my help again. I won't give it next time."

10

ASTRID

Who did he think he was? My fisted hands shook by my sides. He thought he knew everything about my life, but he'd only waltzed into it a day ago.

"'Everything I need.' He has no idea," I muttered beneath my breath as I followed the path toward Steingard. As I crossed a bridge, the dim glow of the sunstones caught my attention. They were beginning to fade in this part of the mountain, which usually took a year after we mined them. I made a mental note to add this bridge to the list of ones that needed replacements.

We had plenty of gems to go around. Whatever power lurked in the tunnel I'd shown Tormund made certain of that. Us dwarves never had to worry about light and heat. And while we enjoyed trading food and drink with sailors beyond the mountain, enough crops grew down here that we could survive without it.

Under the Mountain provided us with everything. Food, water, warmth, light, and shelter. And there were perks on top of that, of course. *Community* was a big one.

The most annoying thing about what Tormund had said was that he was right. I did have everything I needed.

But still, the world beyond called to me. I yearned to feel the sun on my face. Everyone told me the valleys below the mountains were covered in brilliant green grass as soft as a carpet of moss. I wanted to wriggle my toes in it. I wanted to splash in the saltwater sea. Fates, I even wanted to climb a bloomin' tree!

I doubted Tormund had ever climbed a tree in his life.

And what was worse, his brother suffered the same fate, albeit for a different reason.

My stride slowed as I climbed the carved steps leading to the ledge above, daisies lining the path. I did feel for his brother. I truly did. He deserved his freedom just as much as I did, and it didn't seem fair that only one of us could have it.

That wasn't the point, though.

It was that Tormund didn't even *try* to understand why I wanted the bloomin' Everstone so much.

I huffed a breath, taking the last step up to my village's ledge. Why had I even hoped for understanding? Tormund didn't know me. He didn't care. Sure, it felt like we had some common ground now and again, but it was meaningless.

He was probably trying to trick me into seeing him as an ally so I'd happily give up the stone. Not that it was mine to give. Regardless of the weird things going on around here, the gem from Rockheim *had* to be the Everstone. Tormund would eventually win it, then he'd go on his merry way back to Azraak and help his brother.

And I'd still be stuck…here.

I lifted my eyes from the path as my cottage came into view across the bridge. Then I stopped short, startled. My flower boxes were teeming with daisies. Mountainous bunches spilled over the sides of every one and crawled across the ground, twisting like vines up the side of my house. Yulla was out front, her hands windmilling, her face flushed and shining with sweat. My mouth dropped open, and I quickly crossed the bridge to reach her side.

"What in Thor's good name is going on here?" I asked her.

She moaned as she grasped her knees and stood

up straight. Damp strands of hair curled around her red face. "Your flower boxes have exploded."

"Yes, I can see that. But why? What did you feed them earlier?"

It was then I realized *earlier* meant this morning when I'd left to trick Tormund down the spider path. Gods, that felt like five years ago now. So much had happened in such a short amount of time. My quiet little life was usually so much more peaceful. I'd get up, tend to my garden, have a cup of tea, and then head on into work. After work, I'd come home to my silent house, have another cup of tea, and chat with my plants before drifting off to sleep.

Day in, day out. It was nice, even if it was a tad lonely.

"Don't you blame this on me now." She wagged a finger at me. "I fed them the same thing you normally do. It's just water from the Steingard Pond."

Down a tunnel that cut our village in half, we'd found a small pond where natural water trickled in from the cracks in the walls. It was some of the best tasting water in the north, it made my hair feel like silk, and it never ran dry. I was convinced there was something magical about it.

It'd certainly never caused the flowers to do *this*, though.

I scratched the back of my neck. "I suppose I need some more flower boxes."

"You'll need a lot more than that. Look." She pointed at my front door.

I'd shut and locked it before heading to Tormund's camp, and vines burst through the cracks, spilling out onto my front stoop. The two windows facing us were crowded with a bundle of leaves and stems and—I cocked my head—were those more daises?

"All right. What is going on." A statement, rather than a question. It looked like the daisies had gone and taken over my entire house, not that they'd been far off it before.

"Fates if I know." Yulla leaned sideways and tipped her head into my line of sight. She fiddled with her long braid, jingling her bells. "Say, got any more of that chocolate? A bite of it might just help you figure out what you need to do next..."

I slid my eyes from the vines straining against the windowpanes. She grinned at me, the faint lines around her mouth deepening into grooves. I'd always thought those lines said more about her life than she realized. A few years back, she'd lost her husband in a trading accident—his ship had gotten caught up in the Elding, the vicious storm that protected the Isles from intruders. She didn't speak about it much, but I knew from those lines just how happy she'd been. They were like footsteps in the sand. Evidence of how often she'd been there.

I hoped one day she could find something that would deepen those lines even more.

For now, all I could offer her was chocolate. I dug into my tunic and pulled out the remnants of the bar. Half of it was already gone, but I could spare some for an old friend. I snapped off a piece and pressed it into her hand. Then I popped another square into my mouth. The gooey chocolate melted on my tongue. It did in fact make me feel better.

A *bit* better.

"This is more delicious than the last bar Lilia brought you," Yulla mumbled around a mouthful of chocolate.

"So bloomin' delicious, right? I don't think this will calm the plants down, though."

"Well." She propped her fisted hands on her hips. "Should we see what the inside looks like?"

Shrugging, I went over to the door and hauled it open. Vines spilled out onto the front stoop and surrounded my boots within seconds. Yelping, I jumped back before they could snare me in their embrace.

"Hmm," Yulla said from behind me.

I peered inside. The plants had well and truly descended into pure madness. They'd taken up every inch of available space, curling around my dining table, my sofa, and even my barrels of ale. I had a feeling the bed in the loft would be covered, too.

"I don't think I'll have good luck sleeping here tonight." I backed away slowly, my eyes locked on the twitching vines. They seemed to have a mind of their own, and I wasn't about to tempt fate, though their little curling leaves were awfully cute.

"Maybe it's those moss cakes," Yulla said, pointing at the basket still firmly squatting on my dining table. Several vines had curled into the basket, sticking their ends inside the fluffy cakes. Like they were feasting upon the sugary goodness. "You use a different recipe or something?"

"Jostein brought them." I frowned. Tormund's words filled my mind. He was convinced the Everstone was some kind of fake, that someone was tricking the contestants into believing it was real.

Jostein had unveiled the gem. And he'd brought me the moss cakes.

But surely not…Jostein had always looked after me. He looked after *everyone*. There was no bloomin' way he was behind this. Still…it stuck out to me as a strange and unlikely coincidence.

"Well, regardless, you need some place to sleep, but the best I can offer you is a pile of blankets on the floor." She patted me on the back. "You're welcome to that, of course, but I won't be offended if you choose to go elsewhere. I'm sorry I don't have more space."

Yulla and her three children were crammed inside their little cottage. They couldn't carve an expansion because the rock behind their home was the back wall of another cottage, and the chasm sat directly to the left. Anytime I suggested they move, Yulla looked at me like I'd asked her to go the rest of her life without chocolate. She'd lived in that cottage all her life. She wasn't leaving.

"Thanks, Yulla," I replied, "but I don't want to get in the way."

She swatted my arm. "Nonsense. You're always welcome." When I didn't immediately answer, she brushed her hands on her apron and glanced wistfully at her home. "Well, listen. You think about it. If you want a blanket pile tonight, just knock. I'll be up for another hour or two at least."

I smiled. "You're a good friend."

"You best believe it." With a wink, she returned to her cottage. As soon as she vanished through her front door, I turned back to mine. For the first time I could remember, the amount of greenery vastly outweighed the stone. The leaves seemed to glisten beneath the orange glow of the nearby sunstones, and the vines curled toward them as if reaching for the soothing warmth. I couldn't help but smile. It might be an incredible inconvenience, but it sure was pretty.

And so I climbed inside the cracked door, grabbed my pillow and blanket, and returned to my front stoop. This would make as good a spot to sleep as any.

II

ASTRID

The next few days passed in a much more familiar rhythm than those that had come before. I woke as soon as the morning bell signalled dawn, broke fast with Yulla and her family, collected my pickaxe, and went to work in the mines. From morning until late afternoon, I pried the sunstones from the cavern walls and added them to the growing piles. Life was the same as it ever was. The only difference was, I didn't relax at the end of a long day. I returned home and carved into the rock face beside my cottage. It would take me several months to get a new room sorted, but it would be worth it in the end.

Yulla groaned and wiped the sweat from her brow, leaning heavily on her borrowed pickaxe. "I don't know how you do this every day. My body feels like it's been thrown down the chasm. Even my pinky finger hurts."

I smiled and held out a hand for the tool. "You take a break. We've been at this for hours."

"Are *you* going to take a break?" she asked with a meaningful eyebrow arch.

The sunset bell rang well over an hour ago. Many of my neighbors—or at least their children— would soon climb into their beds. Even though I could easily keep going, the crack of my pickaxe against stone would echo through the chasm, keeping the babes awake.

"Don't you worry. I'm stopping now."

"Good." She looked down, frowning at the ever-present pin on my tunic. "And don't forget you have another trial tomorrow."

My mood instantly soured. I'd done my best to put the competition out of my mind, focusing all my energy and effort on mining sunstones and building myself a new home. The plants had well and truly infiltrated my old cottage, but they hadn't expanded beyond that. It had kept me busy enough that Tormund, the Everstone, and all that went with it were out of sight and very much out of mind.

I had not thought of Tormund once.

Not even when I'd lain awake at night, staring

up at the vaulted ceiling and wondering what he was up to in the wait between trials.

Yulla snapped her fingers in front of my eyes. "Don't you dare disappear like that on me while I'm talking to you about the trials. I know you want to pretend they don't exist, but you'll have to participate, whether you like it or not. And you can't zone out when scaling ropes over the chasm."

I swallowed. Yulla was right, of course. I'd watched enough previous competitions to know what came next. We had to cross the chasm by a series of rails, then scale a rope to the top of the mountain, where the watchtower sat. I flexed my hands, wincing at the slight sting from my raw callouses. I'd need to wrap my palms before tomorrow morning, or the ropes would be a problem.

"I'm listening to you. I just…"

"Just take it slowly. You said before you didn't want to win, right?" She shrugged. "So while everyone else is rushing across the rails to get to the rope, you can take the bridge."

The bridge—it was the option for crossing the chasm for anyone who did not feel equipped to handle the rails. But not once had I ever witnessed someone choose the bridge. If you were entering the Fittest Under the Mountain, you'd have trained for this very thing, and you'd feel confident in your ability to make it across.

There were no nets. There were no harnesses or ropes to save you from a fall.

Which was why taking the bridge meant you'd place lower than anyone who didn't, no matter how quickly you made it across.

"Of course I'll take the bridge," I said, heaving a sigh. "But I don't want to think about it any more tonight. It's been a long day. See you in the morning for breakfast?"

Yulla opened her mouth to argue, then seemed to think better of it. "You betcha. Sleep well, Astrid. And don't forget, you have a place at mine if you ever need it."

Yulla wandered back over to her house, and I leaned on the handle of my pickaxe, considering the progress we'd made. After only a few days, we'd made a small indention in the stone. Lilia's partner, Ragnar, had helped a couple of hours every evening, as well as a few others who weren't competing in the trials. Another couple weeks of this, and I might have enough shelter for the cot Jostein had found me. Right now, it perched right beside my flower boxes.

"What happened here?" a voice sounded from behind me.

I whirled, my heart jerking up into my throat.

Tormund stood only a few steps away, arms folded over his chest, brow raised in surprised question. My heart continued to pound. I hadn't seen him for days, and I'd wondered when he'd show his face. I'd begun to think perhaps he never would, that he'd been right about the fake Everstone, that he'd found the real one, and that he'd run back to Azraak without bothering to say, "Ha ha, I win, you lose!"

My pickaxe clattered to the stone floor, and heat flooded my cheeks. I hadn't realized I'd let go of it. "I thought you'd left."

He dragged his gaze from my plant-entombed cottage and cocked his head at me. "Very odd assumption. Not sure what could have given you that idea."

"I haven't seen you for days," I said.

"My friends and I have been preparing for the next trial." His gaze returned to my cottage, then moved on to my new dwelling—what little of it there was. "And you appear to have grown an entire garden that has kicked you out of your own house?"

The mocking tone in his voice made me bristle. "Not that it's any of your business, but...well, yes."

"And instead of trimming these vines so that you can get inside, you're building *another* home?"

He chuckled. "You do have shears, don't you? Why not just make some space?"

I frowned. "Because I don't want to cut them back. Look at them. They're thriving."

He looked at the plants, then looked back at me. A strange expression crossed his face. "You actually mean that, don't you?"

"Well, yes." I gestured emphatically at the world around me. "I don't know if you've noticed, but it's not like we have grass and trees in The Glass Peaks. Few living things survive down here in The Deep. Us and the daises and those vines. I'm not cutting them back, not even a little."

His lips tilted up. "And so you've abandoned your home to them. How long will it take you to build another?"

"Six months, tops, as long as I have some help."

He shook his head. "I thought I hadn't seen you because you were too busy searching for the Everstone."

"I'm not going to find the Everstone."

"You've given up?"

"As unlikely as it seems, I don't think it's a fake," I told him. "And I'll never win the competition, so why hold out any hope? I need to focus on my life here in Steingard, and that life involves a new cottage."

"I see," he replied quietly, almost like he was… disappointed? But that couldn't be the case.

For a moment, neither of us spoke. I didn't know what to say now. As soon as he'd appeared, I'd tensed up, readying myself for some kind of fight. He must have come here before the next trial to rile me up—or at least, that was what I'd expected. He wasn't doing much riling, though.

Suddenly, Yulla poked her head out her open front door. "Hallo! I hate to interrupt, but the children are playing at their friend's house, and I was just about to sit down for dinner. You care to join me?"

I narrowed my gaze at the laughter dancing in her eyes. I could have throttled her. She'd listened to me complain about Tormund for the past three days. Not that I'd had much to say, of course. Just that he was annoying. Mostly I kept quiet where he was concerned. Because I hadn't thought about him at all.

He'd rarely crossed my mind.

"I think Tormund was just on his way back to camp," I said through gritted teeth. "He has a big day tomorrow. What with the competition and all."

But Tormund's face brightened considerably as he said, "A home-cooked meal would be a welcome change. I'd love to join." He pressed his hand to my back. Everything in me tensed. "And for dessert, I have some of that chocolate left. Enough for a square each. What do you say, Astrid? You coming?"

The bastard. I couldn't say no to chocolate, even if it meant sharing a meal with my mortal enemy.

All right, so he wasn't exactly my *mortal enemy*, but I didn't much like him, and he didn't much like me. We were bickering competitors after the same bloomin' object, who begrudgingly spent a day together to hunt for said object. So what exactly did that make us? Not friends or allies, definitely. But not enemies, either. I could never consider someone willing to give me some chocolate an enemy.

Heaving a sigh loud enough for him to hear, I started to walk toward Yulla's house, all too aware of Tormund's hand still pressed against the small of my back.

"So, Tormund," Yulla said, spooning some buttered potatoes onto each plate, "Astrid tells me you're from Azraak."

Tormund shot me a wicked smile, and my stomach turned. "Astrid has been talking about me, has she?"

"She's had quite a lot to say." Yulla laughed. "Not all of it was good, mind you."

"Yulla," I warned.

She plopped some mushrooms onto my plate and frowned. "What? You told me he knew how much he annoys you."

I dropped my head into my hands, mostly to obscure how red my cheeks must be. They were flaming hot.

Tormund laughed. "The feeling is mutual, for the most part."

For the most part? I lifted my head but focused my attention on my very full plate. Yulla had cooked up a feast of potatoes, mushrooms, smoked fish, and moss chips. *For the most part*, my mind repeated to me. So, I didn't entirely annoy him? There were parts of him that felt a different way? But what parts? And what was the other feeling?

"Azraak is cold and dark, but it can be quite lovely during the winter months," Tormund began, as if he hadn't just said something incredibly outlandish about his parts not being annoyed by me. "Visitors love the hot springs in particular."

Yulla leaned forward, clasping her hands together. "Oh, I would love to visit the hot springs. I bet you use them all the time. I sure would if I lived there."

"I find them uncomfortable." Tormund gestured

at the shadowy strands curling around his arms. "My body likes darkness and shadows, not hot places."

Yulla nodded. "I've heard that. I suppose it must have been quite the journey for you to come here this time of year. It's still only spring, but it gets hot outside."

"It was worth it," he said quietly. "I swore to my brother I'd compete this year, and I've yet to break a promise to him."

She leaned forward and patted his arm. "Good man."

I narrowed my eyes, an argument on the tip of my tongue. But that argument quickly vanished. As grudging as I was to admit it, Tormund had his merits. He cared for his family. He'd journeyed far to help his brother, devoted to his cause. Yes, he'd antagonized me, but I'd antagonized him right back. So, in reality, he kind of...*was* a good man. I'd never tell him that, though.

"Good demon," he replied, winking at Yulla.

"How could I forget with your horns hitting my sunstone lamp every time you move?"

Tormund straightened in surprise, clearly unaware that he kept bashing her sunstones. And in his jolting, he hit the lamp again. "I'm so sorry. I had no idea."

"Bad demon," she said.

Tormund stared at her for a moment, then broke out into laughter.

A slow grin spread across Yulla's face. I shook my head and smiled. It was one of the oddest dinners I'd ever experienced, but the memory of it would last a lifetime.

12

TORMUND

Astrid and I stood in the middle of the bridge spanning the chasm. Her eyes were bright, her cheeks pink. It was from the glow of the sunstones and a belly full of fresh food. And hopefully good company, I had to admit. Happiness looked good on her.

"You ready for tomorrow?" I asked, sliding my hands into my pockets. I'd thought little of the competition throughout dinner. Strange, when it had invaded my thoughts almost every waking moment of every single day for at least the past six months.

"Not particularly," she admitted with a tinkling laugh. "You?"

"Pretty particularly," I admitted right back.

"Contrary to your assumptions about me, I researched the fates out of the trials before coming here. This next one was fairly easy to replicate back home. I spent four months practicing it."

"Right. Well, I should have guessed you were downplaying your knowledge the other day," she replied. "To contrast that, I have spent exactly zero hours preparing."

"Well, that's a very blatant lie, Astrid Balstad."

A rosy flush went through her cheeks, dotting the end of her nose. "I assure you it's not. You have nothing to worry about when it comes to me. I plan on taking the bridge."

I furrowed my brow. "But then you'll come last unless someone else decides to take it, too."

"I am very aware. Thank you, Tormund."

"You're a *miner*," I said. "Look at those bloody arms of yours."

She twisted her arms around her back, as if to hide them from me. "I would really rather not. The shape of them has always bothered me." Then that rosiness deepened another shade into crimson. "I don't know why I'm saying this to you. I think it's time for bed."

Gently, I wrapped my hand around her forearm and tugged her hand out from behind her back. Her shapely arms filled her shirt, curves as enticing as her ample hips and thighs. "You have beautiful arms, Astrid. They're strong and powerful. You should be proud of them and what they can do for you."

She swallowed and looked away. "I suppose I've never really thought of them that way."

"Trust me when I say you should." Suddenly, the urge to run my fingers up her arm and rest them against her neck shot through me like a bolt of lightning. I blinked and stepped back, releasing my grip on her. What in fate's name was getting into me? I couldn't entertain those kinds of thoughts, least of all for her. Meral was happy enough to engage in flings and short-term affairs, but that had never been my thing. Relationships in general never had been. I didn't like to get attached, even if temporarily. Romance with me would only ever end in heartache—or worse.

Besides, Astrid would gladly shove me off this bridge if it meant she could have the one thing I needed more than anything else.

But...that wasn't quite true, was it? We were standing here now, and she showed no signs of anger. Just...defeated resignation. She'd given up on the Everstone. Not only would she give little effort to the competition, but I doubted she'd even search the mines for it now.

I should be happy. She wouldn't stand in my way. The only people I had to worry about now were the trio of competitors who'd come closest to beating Galinn the Great in previous years, though they'd never been much of a threat to him.

And yet, I wanted to urge her to actually *try*.

Astrid tipped back her head to look up at me. "Why are you here, Tormund? Are you after something? I told you where I thought I'd find the Everstone."

"I came tonight because I wanted to know what you were up to. I stayed because dinner sounded nice. And wasn't it?"

"Nice?" She opened her mouth, and I could tell she wanted to say it hadn't been. But then she sighed. "Yes, I suppose it was nice. Do you often make it a habit of dining with your enemies the eve before battle?"

And then words fell out of my head and off my tongue before I could stop them. "When they're as pretty as you, yes."

Astrid bit her bottom lip. My eyes snagged on where her tooth dug into her pink skin. Gods be good.

"I told you flattery will get you nowhere with me," she said, but her voice was a pitch softer than it had been before.

"Then I suppose I shouldn't tell you that I can't

wait to see how brilliant you are at swinging across those rails." I took a few steps back and winked. Time to get out of here before I got myself into trouble. Because this was starting to feel a bit too much like trouble. Astrid and her flowing ginger hair decorated with bells, her big beautiful eyes, those curves—*trouble*.

"I told you I'm taking the bridge," she called after me.

"Good night, Astrid." With another wink, I turned and forced myself to walk away.

"Where have you been?" Altan asked from where he paced beside the campfire. He slowed to a stop and scowled at me. "I thought you'd gotten lost in the mines. I was about to ask the dwarves to ring their bloody alarm bell."

I held up my hands. "I went to dinner."

"Dinner?" Meral glanced up from the book propped open on her legs. "With who?"

Altan shot her a frank look. "Come on. I think we all know who."

"Good point," said Meral.

"What's that supposed to mean?" I asked.

"You've been talking about the lass for three

bloody days," Meral said, shaking her head and returning her attention to her book. "Who else would it be? You're practically pining over her."

"I'm not pining over her. I don't even like her!"

Meral snorted. "All right. If that's what you need to tell yourself."

"I don't," I said. But that was a lie. I'd realized that tonight. "Well, I suppose I do, but there's no pining involved here. I just like her the same way I like you two. She's a decent person and very good at what she does, whether she realizes it or not. Plus, she's enjoyable to be around. There's something about her laugh and her eyes and her presence that's—what?"

Meral was outright grinning at me over the top of her book. "You like her the same way you like us, huh? I didn't know you tended to wax poetic about my eyes." She fluttered her lashes at me. "Do you want to dive into the deep blue waters of them or—"

I snatched the book out of her hands and held it over the flames. Meral squeaked.

"What was that?" I asked.

"You wouldn't," she said, her eyes widening.

"Oh, I would."

Altan sauntered over and perched on the log beside Meral. He elbowed her, then pointed at me.

"If he didn't like her, he wouldn't give a rat's arse that we were bugging him about her."

"You have a point," said Meral, "but I would like to finish reading that book. I just got to the part where the warrior has ridden into battle against the enemy. I need to know if she wins."

"She wins," I said, waving the book over the fire. "They always win."

She leapt to her feet. "Give me back my book!"

I grinned. "It's so easy to get a rise out of you. You have to know I'd never burn one of these things." Then I tossed it back over. She caught it with a single hand and immediately settled back onto the log with her nose between the pages.

As I turned toward my tent, Meral called out, "Nice job distracting us, Tormund. But we know you've got a soft spot for the girl now. Hope you don't forget why you came here."

I slowed, but I didn't turn around.

"Stay focused on the task," Altan added. "We're here for Tahir. If we don't get our hands on that gem, he'll never go above ground. And I know that girl wants it, too. You know you can't get involved. It'll only end in heartache."

Altan was right, of course, and he was using my own words to make his point. I'd told him time and time again I didn't want romance in my life. Astrid was a distraction. A very pretty distraction. And if I wasn't careful, I might lose sight of my quest. I had to keep a reasonable distance from now on. No more dinners. No more late-night goodbyes on chasm bridges. She was a fellow competitor, which meant she could never be anything more than a friend.

13

ASTRID

"Welcome to the second trial of this year's Fittest Under the Mountain!" Jostein's booming voice echoed through the wide chasm yawning before us, the darkness below an impenetrable black that felt like an endless nothingness.

I swallowed and stared down. It was one thing to traverse our dwarven-built bridges, lined as they were with stone railings embedded with sunstones. And it was quite another to tiptoe across the rickety wooden planks bouncing around in the breeze. I didn't even want to think about the metal rungs looping from one side to the next, but every other contestant had lined up behind the start position for those.

I was the only one who'd chosen the bridge.

Still, sweat coated my palms like I'd gone for the alternative.

Spectators crowded onto every ledge lining the chasm, cheering and waving their multi-colored banners. Even here, the roar was deafening. Lilia caught my eye from the ledge just across, but she was deep in conversation with Ragnar and another elf—a silver-haired man with an uncanny resemblance to her—and an orcish woman. I squinted. She was powerfully built and graceful in the way she moved. That must be Lilia's brother, Rivelin, and his partner, Daella. But Lilia had told me he didn't much like leaving his little village over on Hearthaven. And by the furrow of his brow, he didn't seem thrilled to be here, either.

The cheers suddenly hushed, and a murmur went through the crowd.

Jostein's hands had fallen to his sides, and an eerie white sheen stained his face. The two visitors from Rockheim stood beside him, feverishly whispering into his ear. With every moment that passed, the whites of his knuckles grew whiter.

"What do you think that's about?" a voice said —right into my ear. I leapt and released a rather undignified yelp, then whirled to glare at Tormund. He'd sneaked up on me again.

"You really need to make more noise when you

move. One of these times, you're going to make my heart fall out of my chest."

For once, laughter didn't dance in his eyes. He was too focused on Jostein's pale face, which was, undeniably, concerning. "Those two have come bearing very bad news."

"Well spotted," I told him.

He finally turned to face me. "Why are you so grumpy this morning?"

"As if you don't know," I replied crisply.

"Is this about me being quiet earlier?"

I'd arrived at the competition platform half an hour early. Tormund had been the only other contestant to do the same. After last night's dinner, I'd expected a hearty hello. Or at least a friendly one. We'd share a meal, some laughs, and then a goodbye that had felt like the beginning of a friendship of sorts. But when I'd told him hello, he'd given me a curt nod and then proceeded to ignore me until everyone else had arrived.

"It was very rude," I pointed out. "You didn't even say hello."

"Now that's not true. I said hello."

"You absolutely did not," I argued.

He folded his arms. "I gave you a nod."

"A nod is not hello. It's less than hello. It's a very rude way of dismissing someone. What happened to everything you said last night?"

Knut stuck his head between us, his black bushy beard wobbling, his brow arched high. "What happened last night?"

"Nothing!" Tormund and I nearly shouted in unison.

Tormund caught my eye. I rolled mine at him. Then we both cracked grins simultaneously.

"All right, all right." Knut held up his hands. "You keep on doing whatever it is you're doing if you want, but Jostein looks really unhappy. And I think it has something to do with the Everstone."

My head snapped Jostein's way. The old dwarven man was wringing his hands, his eyes darting across the competitors. When they landed on my face, his lips twisted down, and he sighed. My heart thumped. There would only be one reason for an expression like that.

He hurried over to the nine of us. "I'm afraid I have some unfortunate news. The Everstone is, ah, missing."

I pressed my lips together.

Altan, one of Tormund's friends, barked, "Missing?"

"I am afraid so."

"But how?" Knut asked.

Jostein winced. "We locked it inside a crate in the back room of The Wet Beard. When we checked on things this morning, we found that someone had smashed open the crate."

"A wooden crate?" Tormund asked, his voice lethally calm.

Jostein nodded.

"Not the most secure of compartments, is it? Especially not when most of the people here own multiple pickaxes."

Jostein's eyes went ice cold. "I didn't anticipate anyone would wish to steal something from us. The only times we've experienced theft have been when *visitors* come for the trials."

Tormund folded his arms and lifted his chin. "I don't like what you're implying."

"I heard you're keen to get your hands on the Everstone," said Jostein. "You came here especially for it."

"That's right," Tormund replied. "And if I'd stolen it, I'd be long gone by now."

Jostein took a step closer to Tormund, puffing out his chest, which only resulted in making his beard bounce around some more.

"Stop it, you two," I said, stepping between them. To Jostein, I said, "This must be a mistake. You said this happened at The Wet Beard? I'll go take a look and sort this out, all right?"

Jostein frowned. "You must stay and compete in the trial."

"The Everstone is the prize," I countered. "We can't continue with the games until we find it."

A pause. "All right. I can see your point. But what in fate's name am I going to tell them?" He lifted his gaze to scan the silent crowd. They were all waiting for some kind of signal that everything was fine and that the games would continue without delay. Most looked forward to these events all year. He would have some disappointing news to deliver.

"I don't think you should mention the missing Everstone yet," I said. "If hundreds find out, hundreds will start searching for it. And if everyone clogs The Wet Beard, it'll just be chaos."

"Then what do we tell them?" he asked.

"I have an idea. Say Astrid twisted her foot. The trials will resume once her ankle's all wrapped up." Tormund shot me a wolfish smile. Alarm rattled through me. Before I could brace myself, he swept me up in his arms and carted me away.

"**P**ut me down!" I swatted Tormund's arm. He hummed to himself, practically prancing down the tunnel toward The Wet Beard. He hadn't said a word since we'd left the crowded ledges behind, and I was starting to get a little annoyed. All right, *a lot* annoyed.

"You can put me down now," I said through clenched teeth. "No one can see us anymore, and I am perfectly capable of—eep!"

Tormund tossed me over his shoulder, my boots now up in the air, my head bouncing against his back. "What was that, Astrid? I couldn't hear you over the sound of my own laughter."

"Amazing. I'm glad you're getting so much amusement out of this." I poked him in the back. Gods, there were muscles there, too! "If you don't put me down, I'll tell everyone you're the gem thief."

He slowed, sighed, and lowered me. As soon as my feet hit the ground, I brushed off my tunic and danced several steps away from him. "You *didn't* steal it, though, right?"

"No, I didn't steal it," said Tormund. "Did you?"

"I haven't been to The Wet Beard in days."

"Is that a no? Because you're the first person I'd suspect."

"Yes, of course it's a no. And *you're* the first person *I'd* suspect. You're telling me you wouldn't steal it if you knew where it was?"

A beat passed before he answered. "I'd be tempted. But I didn't know it was there, so I didn't do it. Someone else did. If that's even the stone. I'm still not convinced it is."

"Well, regardless," I told him, "something is missing from The Wet Beard, and I promised Jostein I'd look into it. If I return to the chasm now, he'll probably start the trial, even without the prize. The dwarves won't like that he's stalling. Truth be told, I'm surprised he let us walk away. He usually has a 'the trials must go on no matter what' kind of attitude."

Tormund fell into step beside me as I continued down the tunnel. "You were pretty eager to get away from there."

"If it wasn't obvious, I don't want to compete. I was the only one who chose the bridge."

"You could have chosen to swing across the metal rails."

"Too dangerous," I said. "I'm not strong enough."

"Astrid Balstad." Tormund grabbed my arm and tugged me to a stop. When I allowed my feet to slow, he stepped in front of me, blocking my path. "What's it going to take for you to believe in yourself?"

The intensity of his stare made me swallow. "I'm just being practical."

He stepped closer, invading my space, and tucked a crooked finger beneath my chin. "Say something like that one more time, and I'll carry you the rest of the way to the tavern."

"You're such a bastard," I said with a laugh.

"Yes." He smiled. "And that's why you like me."

"I *don't* like you," I protested. But he'd already moved away and was halfway down the tunnel now. With a frustrated sigh, I jogged to catch up to him. As if he'd not just threatened to toss me back on his shoulder, he sauntered around the bend and strode right up to the arched doorway leading into The Wet Beard.

All was silent and empty inside.

It was eerie, seeing it like this. Everyone was at the competition, leaving the place full of shadows and cobwebs. It felt unusually dark and dreary without the raucous laughter, the stomping of feet, and the pluck of strings on a bard's lute.

Tormund frowned and pointed at the dim sunstones. "Aren't they usually brighter than this?"

"When they're freshly lit, yes," I answered. "But that's why we have to keep mining sunstones. Their magic doesn't last forever. We have to replace them every year or so."

"Right." Tormund moved down the length of the tavern. I cast a furtive glance at the bar, where no one stood ready and waiting to pour another ale. Balder would be spectating along with everyone else, though he'd likely hurry back now that Jostein had called off the trial. He'd want to be ready when the crowd descended on the place—and they would.

"A bit odd, eh?" Tormund called over his shoulder.

"Yeah, I've never been in here when it's empty like this," I said, following him to the door that led to the back office, where the Everstone had been stored.

"No, I mean all the sunstones. They're dimming at the same time."

I looked around and could have sworn it was darker in the tavern than it had been a moment before. "Hmm. Well, if all these sunstones were mined on the same day, it isn't particularly odd. They'll run out of magic around the same time."

"You're a miner," he countered. "Were they mined on the same day?"

"I don't know. I usually do the bridges." I frowned. "Why are you hung up on this? The sunstones run out. It's nothing unusual."

"*Everything* related to this stolen gem is unusual."

"Including you?" I asked.

A smile curled his lips as his palm hit the back door. "Excellent observation."

Tormund shoved open the door, and we both

inched into a small room with a sloped stone ceiling, also embedded with dying sunstones. The dim lighting revealed a small desk, a rack stacked with tankards and wine goblets, and a smashed crate large enough to house the Everstone. Tormund knelt beside the crate and cocked his head, like the very sight of it might give him enough insight into what exactly happened here.

But there wasn't much to see. It was just an ordinary wooden crate, smashed to bits. But something wriggled in the back of my mind—a thought, something almost too opaque for me to grasp. I had the sudden urge to take a few steps back and look at the door again.

Leaving Tormund beside the crate, I edged into the main part of the tavern. Black char curled around the doorframe. Some of the wood was even blackened and bent. Like someone had taken flames to it.

Interesting, since Balder didn't even have a hearth here.

Tormund suddenly tensed and snatched something from the floor, then he slowly looked up and met my gaze through the open door.

"What is that?" I asked in a whisper.

He held it up. A black talon gleamed in the dimming glow of the tavern. It was as large as

Tormund's hand. "This belongs to some kind of creature. One of your spider friends, perhaps?"

"No, I don't think so." I swallowed, glancing back at the char. "If I were to guess, that's from a dragon."

14

ASTRID

"If there's a dragon in the mines, don't you think we should go straight to Jostein about it?" Tormund asked, still eyeing the talon. Balder had arrived only a few moments later, and Tormund had whisked the claw out of sight. But now that we were back at my cottage, he'd brought it back out again.

I'd asked him to give me a moment to think before we decided what to do about it. But at least an hour had passed since then, and I was no closer to knowing than I had been before.

"I am on the fence about that," was my reply.

"A dragon who now has the power of the Everstone?" Tormund looked up. "Sounds like a dangerous combination."

"Look at the size of that talon," I told him. "It's barely as big as your hand."

"You make my hands sound small," he countered. "I can assure you, they are plenty large enough, just like the rest of me."

I blinked, my chest warming. "I'm going to choose to ignore the last part of that comment. But yes, while you are—"

"Big." He grinned.

I rolled my eyes. "Dragons are supposed to be incredible, majestic beings."

"Are you saying I'm not majestic?"

"Can we please focus on the task at hand?"

"I don't know." His smile widened. "Are you able to focus, or am I too distracting? Is it my big hands? Don't think I haven't noticed you keep looking at them."

"I am looking at the *talon*." I cleared my throat. Truth was, he'd caught me. I *had* been looking at his hands, but only to measure the size of the talon. I hadn't been wondering what exactly he meant by *big*. Or what else might be even larger. "What I'm trying to say is that a full-grown dragon's talon would be much larger than that. This one belongs to an adolescent."

"All right. That seems possible. I'm not sure where you're going with this, however."

"Well, I don't want anyone to hurt him. Or her," I said.

Tormund's lips quirked up in the corners. "You want to protect the dragon—the one who stole your coveted Everstone."

"I mean, according to you, it's a fake, so."

"And you don't believe it is?" He cocked a brow.

"I don't see what anyone would get out of it."

"Get out of what?" Jostein asked as his boots tapped the stone path. He came to a stop a few feet away, his wide eyes surveying the mess of vines. "You still haven't trimmed these plants?"

"That's why I started carving out a new space," I said, jerking my thumb toward the abandoned pickaxe and the small curve in the wall.

He shook his head. "Nevermind that. Did you find anything at the tavern?"

"No," I said tightly, then gently elbowed Tormund's side.

He grinned up at Jostein. "Just a lot of ale. Say, you ever think about putting a hearth in the tavern? It'd be nice and cozy to have some *fire* in—ow!"

"Oh, sorry," I chirped, removing my elbow from his side. "Didn't realize how close you were."

Jostein frowned. "Well, I can't say I've ever

thought about it seeing as the tavern isn't mine. I'll make the suggestion to Balder, but I can already tell you his answer. He'll say there's not enough space, and he'd rather have the bard stage than a hearth. But nevermind all that. You really didn't find anything?"

"I suppose it was only wishful thinking," I said quickly. "I mean, you'd already searched for answers, too, right?"

He heaved a sigh and ran his fingers through his beard. "I'd just hoped you'd spot something I'd missed. You've always had a keen eye for detail."

"I agree," Tormund piped up. "Astrid here does notice details others do not. Such as the size of things."

"Will you stop it?" I hissed at him.

"What's this about, then?" Jostein asked.

Tormund opened his mouth to speak, but I cut him off. There was no telling what he'd spout next. "He's just annoyed the competition has been put on hold, and he's blaming me for it."

"I'm sorry, lad," Jostein said, awkwardly patting Tormund's shoulder. "I'd reschedule the trial for tomorrow night, but everyone's feeling uneasy about the missing gem. Once we sort that out, we can get everything back on track."

"And if no one finds it?" Tormund asked.

"Well." Jostein tugged on the end of his beard. "I suppose there'll be no more competition until next year. We'll just have to throw a party instead. Don't worry—I can promise you it'll be quite the festival if it comes to that."

Jostein clapped his hands together and started rattling off things to plan like he'd already given up on finding the Everstone. I didn't blame him. Rockheim took in prisoners from other islands, who were promptly put to work, but we here in the north didn't have much by way of warriors or guards. We'd never needed them, for the most part. The fact we had to track down a thief felt as foreign as the faraway lands of Azraak.

After asking us to inform him if we came upon any clues at all, Jostein eventually wandered off, knocking on nearby doors to tell my neighbors the same. His voice drifted toward us, echoing down the chasm. He was already telling people there was going to be a party.

"You're really not going to tell him about the talon?" Tormund murmured.

"No." I shook my head. "At least not yet."

"Then what, pray tell, do you plan to do in the meantime?"

I leaned closer to whisper into his ear, my head bumping against the base of his horns. "I want to find the dragon."

Unfortunately, the dragon hunting would have to wait until the morning. Lilia and Ragnar descended upon my humble abode only moments later, and then Yulla ventured out of her cottage to see what all the fuss was about. They wanted to know everything. And then they wanted to cheer me up about the end of the competition, even though they all knew I'd rather curl up in my house with a mug of tea and my plants rather than traipse across a rickety bridge.

The fact that the Everstone was missing was enough. Most of the dwarves down in The Deep didn't know the details of my curse, but Yulla did. And Lilia, of course. They dragged me from my front stoop and deposited me on a chair at The Wet Beard, then shoved a tankard into my hands.

A bard was already at it, wailing a tune about an orcish woman's year-long quest through the mountains, searching for a hoard of gold. Along the way, she met all manner of folk: elves and pixies and even mountain trolls. At every stop, she collected a new companion until she had thirty others travelling with her. She never found that hoard of gold, but when she left the mountains, she felt she didn't need it anymore. She'd found something far more valuable. Kinship, a family of her choosing, a home.

By the end of the song, Lilia had a tear in her eye, which she brushed away before anyone saw it other than me. When I caught her in the act, she gave me a wry smile. "Beautiful story, eh? I love a happy ending."

"You're such a hopeless romantic." I clinked my tankard against hers. "To happy endings." I inclined my head toward Ragnar, who'd gotten into an energetic conversation about knives with Balder, who didn't know the first thing about blades. Still, he seemed eager to be involved in a conversation that had nothing to do with ale.

Lilia tapped her drink against mine. "I hope you find yours."

I took a long gulp of the ale before answering. "That's less likely now that someone has stolen the Everstone."

I hadn't mentioned the dragon to her yet, though I would as soon as I could tug her away from the tavern. Out of everyone, Lilia would understand the most. She'd want to protect the dragon, too. And she might have some idea on how best to find one lurking in dwarven mines.

She cocked her head. "I'm not sure you need the Everstone to get your happy ending. You and Tormund seem to be getting along well."

Heat crept up my neck. "I don't hate him anymore, but that's as far as it goes."

"I don't think he hates you anymore, either," she said with a wink.

"Yes, non-hatred. That's a fantastic foundation for a relationship."

Shrugging, she gazed adoringly at her man. "Ragnar really annoyed me when I first met him. Well, that's not quite true. We hit it off, but then he tried to steal my business from me."

I arched a brow. "Your Travelling Tavern business?"

"That's right." Her tinkling laugh warmed me from head to toe. "But it turned out there was more to his story than I knew. He won me over in the end."

"Well, I know Tormund's story," I told her. "He already shared it."

"And did you share your story with him?"

"You know I can't do that. It was hard enough getting you to guess it."

"He seems clever. I'm sure you can lead him to the same realization I had. Oh!" Suddenly, she sat back and swung her gaze behind me. There was only one reason she would look like that. Tormund had appeared. The heat in my cheeks flamed up a notch. Even though I doubted he'd overheard our conversation, I felt like I'd been caught red-handed.

If he knew I'd been talking about him…and not in a negative way, either…he'd be absolutely bloomin' unbearable.

But I hadn't said anything embarrassing. All I'd admitted was that I didn't dislike him. That was hardly a declaration of interest. And I *wasn't* interested.

He grabbed a stool and sat beside me, the scent of leather and musk washing over me. Gods, he smelled good. I blinked and took a drag of my ale.

"Having a nice time?" he asked us.

"I always love an evening spent inside a tavern." Lilia lifted her tankard and waved it around. Her eyes were a little glassy. She was accustomed to drinking her ale, but Balder's brew was much stronger—eye-wateringly so at times. Hers was sweet and led to a buzzy, tipsy head. Balder's tended to get people drunk.

Tormund palmed the table and grinned. "Me, too. I'm going to request a song from the bard. Are there any in particular you'd like to hear?"

He directed the question at me, but I was so busy staring into my empty tankard that Lilia answered for me. "Oh, there's a great one about a mountain troll I haven't heard in months. Ask the bard if she knows it!"

"Is it upbeat?" he asked.

"Very."

"Good." Tormund stood and held out a hand. He angled it just enough that I couldn't miss it, what with his palm stuck over the rim of my tankard. "Would you like to dance, Astrid?"

I swallowed around the lump in my throat and braced myself. When I looked up at him, I suddenly forgot why I felt so on edge. I also couldn't remember why I'd found him so obnoxiously irritating when we'd first met. Because the heat in his eyes now tugged me to my feet. And as I followed after him, I felt like I was seeing him for who he really was—not the sauntering, smug bastard who'd rolled in here ready to steal the win from everyone else. Tormund was a man—a demon —who'd do anything for those he loved. And for that, I could not dislike him. Not even a little bit.

In fact, I liked that about him quite a lot.

And that was when I realized I was a little bit drunk but also in trouble.

I liked Tormund. And he was pulling me onto the dance floor.

15

TORMUND

It was a miracle Astrid had agreed to join me for a dance. For a moment, I thought she'd refuse. She'd barely been able to look at me, staring into her empty tankard and likely cursing my name. Before I'd shown up, she'd had a quiet, cozy life. But now, conspiracies were afoot, and dragons were stealing fake gems. It was all too much of a coincidence. At first, I'd thought it was connected to her, but I'd been wrong. All this had something to do with me, and she'd likely guessed that by now.

The talon was a warning, specifically targeted at me.

Someone must have found out my secret. The brother I wanted to save wasn't a shadow demon.

He wasn't even my brother. He was a dragon.

I asked the bard for Lilia's song, and the winged pixie erupted into a very vigorous, upbeat tune about mountain trolls. With Astrid's hand in mine, I spun us across the floor. Other than Jostein and his partner, a dwarven woman short in stature and curvy in hips, we were the only two making use of the dance area.

Astrid looked up at me through thick, dark lashes that I swore looked as soft as feathers. "I should have known you like to dance when no one else is. You seem to like showing off your skills."

"Ah but there you've got me wrong." I smiled. "When I dance, no one else exists except my partner."

Astrid glanced away, and her face went pink. No other barbs emerged from her luscious lips, though I found myself holding my breath in anticipation, in case she'd needed a moment to think of something good. But then I remembered why I'd brought her out here. And it wasn't to dance. Or get distracted by her lips, for fate's sake.

I inclined my head toward Jostein as we spun past him and his wife. "They were having an intense conversation earlier, then they took to the dance floor."

She jerked her head toward them, and a look of sudden realization crossed her face. "You want to overhear what they're saying? That's why you wanted to dance."

I had the sudden urge to tell her she was wrong, but that would be a lie. One I couldn't afford to tell based on the disappointment that flickered through her eyes. There was something between us. It was impossible to ignore now. But I couldn't explore what could be—it would always have to be what could have been.

I had to find the Everstone, take it for myself, and return to Azraak alone. There was no other option. She and I could never be more than…whatever this was.

Still, I found myself winking in her direction. It was like my damn body had a mind of its own. "I'd also never say no to a dance with a beautiful woman, though it's been a long time. Back in Azraak, celebrations like this are few and far between, but when we celebrate, we *really* celebrate. You should come to our winter feast one year. It's one not to be missed."

I expected a laugh—or a retort, at the very least—but she pulled out of my arms and backed away. "I think I'm going to call it a night."

"What? Why?" I reached for her, but she shook her head and walked off, vanishing out the tavern's front door.

Lilia suddenly appeared before me, her silver brow furrowed. "What did you just say to her?"

I held up my hands. "All I did was tell her she's beautiful."

"And that's it?" Frowning, she glanced over her shoulder at where her friend had disappeared.

"That and I suggested she come to Azraak's winter feast one year. Nothing untoward, I swear to you."

Lilia sighed. "Ah, that was it, then."

I frowned. "The feast part?"

"Yes, you silly demon." She turned back toward me, shaking her head. "Haven't you figured it out by now? Astrid's curse? She is bound to this mountain, which means she's trapped here for her entire life. Astrid can never visit Azraak. There are no winter feasts in her future."

Realization crashed down on me, and suddenly, everything Astrid had said and done tore through my mind. She had been so understanding about my 'brother's' affliction. She'd looked so wistful every time she'd mentioned the world outside. Just like Tahir, she was a prisoner in her own home. And just like Tahir, she dreamt of spreading her wings to fly.

"Ah," I said.

Lilia nodded. "Ah."

"The Everstone can free her."

"That's right. And now it's missing. But what's more important is *you*." She gave me a pointed look. "Whether she realizes it or not, she likes you. I can tell by the way she looks at you. And you seem to like her, too. What are you going to do about it, Tormund? You could make her a very happy woman if you chose to do so."

My heart pounded my ribs; my mouth went dry. "You're asking me to let her have the Everstone. That's not fair."

"It's not fair that the one person she might actually like is the one person who would keep the gem from her if he got his hands on it."

I blew out a breath. "I don't want it for myself. It's for my brother. Besides…" Grinding my teeth, I glanced away. "Astrid and I can't have a connection. Once this is all over, I'm returning home to Azraak. Alone."

"You'll change your mind. You know how I know that?" Lilia asked, sliding sideways to catch my eyes again. "Because Astrid is a catch. She's an incredible woman, good at what she does and endlessly kindhearted. And there's not a doubt in my mind you've seen all that, too. So go find that Everstone and give it to her."

Lilia walked away, right into the arms of the crimson-haired elf she'd partnered with. He drew her in close, nuzzling her ear. Lilia returned the affection by tilting back her head and gifting him a beaming smile as bright as the stars. Happiness practically rolled off their bodies in waves. An unexpected twinge of longing went through me. I'd never had something like that.

And I never would.

Until now, I'd never really wanted it.

I blinked and looked away. Even if I let down my walls, none of it would matter. Tahir needed the Everstone, and I couldn't fail him. Astrid would never forgive me when I took it from her, cursing her to remain inside these mountainous walls for the rest of her life. Because that was what I'd be doing. Letting the curse remain hers forever.

She would hate me as long as she lived. And I wouldn't blame her for it.

16

I half-expected Tormund to follow me back home. And when he never materialized from the shadows, I didn't know whether to be relieved or disappointed. Perhaps a little of both. As soon as he'd started talking about Azraak, I'd only been reminded of how tenuous our friendship was. At the end of the day, we needed the same thing, and neither of us would back down. He wanted freedom for his brother, and I needed freedom for myself.

When I reached my vine-engulfed cottage, I tugged the cot further into the new build and climbed on top without bothering to change into more comfortable clothes. My bones were weary, and my eyelids were weighed down by stones. But despite my exhaustion, I tossed and turned all night. I couldn't get the vision of Tormund's midnight eyes out of my mind—or how his hands had felt wrapped around me.

At least it gave me time to make a plan.

After I tumbled out of bed and splashed some cool water on my face, I stuffed some supplies into my pack and took off toward the mines. The answer had come to me, and it was simple enough. I would track down the dragon by myself and use the Everstone's power before Tormund even knew I'd gone anywhere.

I'd left a note at my cottage, saying I'd decided to practice for the upcoming trial, for when or if the competition started again. It was a believable enough lie, and I'd refrained from specifying which trial I meant and where I'd be training. I hoped that Tormund would go looking for me, and he'd waste the entire day trying to figure out where I was.

By the time he realized the note was a lie, I'd have returned from my quest all curse-free and happy as a clam.

Perfect plan!

As I traipsed across the bridge, the sunstones dimmed. Frowning, I noticed all the gems embedded along the bridge were quickly fading. I'd swapped these out myself a few weeks ago. They shouldn't be losing their shine just yet.

The ones in The Wet Beard had faded, too. Seemed like an odd coincidence.

No matter. It could wait until I got back.

Not much later, I waltzed into the back end of the mine tunnel, avoiding the usual entrance, where dozens of dwarves would be starting their mining duties for the day. I wanted to avoid any questions about why I'd taken the day off work and why I carried a packed bag.

When I walked inside, an eerie darkness enveloped me. Most of the sunstones here had gone out, even though they'd yet to be pried from the stone walls. An uneasy thump went through my heart, and I stopped to stare. Not once had I ever seen a sunstone lose its glow before being mined. As long as they remained embedded in their natural walls, they shined for years. They only began to lose their power when we interfered.

My gut churned. Something wasn't right.

The shadows parted, and Tormund emerged from the darkness. I yelped and danced back, the hammering of my heart so painful I had to grasp my shirt. "For Thor's bloomin' sake, Tormund. You can't appear out of thin air like that. If I had a pickaxe on me, I would have swung it at your head before I knew it was you."

"I followed you."

"'Course you did." I threw up my hands, annoyed that I hadn't seen it coming. He'd probably already guessed I'd go for the dragon after what I'd said to him last night. How long had he waited for me to sneak off? I wanted to throw something at him for it, but I had to admit I'd have done the same thing if I were him.

He eyed the straps of my bag tightened around my shoulders. Coolly, he asked, "Going somewhere?"

"You know exactly where I'm going."

"To find the dragon."

"I thought I'd make friends with the beast."

"You thought you'd find the Everstone without me," he countered.

A beat passed before I replied. "Do you blame me?"

"Not in the least." Shoving his hands into his pockets, he turned toward the sunstones I'd been inspecting. With his back turned my way, I could see he'd had the same idea I'd had. He wore a satchel, so stuffed that the linen material strained against the contents, threads unravelling.

"You know, for someone who thinks the

missing gem is a fake, you're very intent on finding it," I said.

He pointed at the wall. "Is that normal?"

"The faded sunstones? Not in the least." I moved in front of him, though all that accomplished was getting myself trapped between the wall and his chest. "They don't go out until many months after we mine them."

"Bit odd, isn't it?" he asked.

"Very." I took off down the mine tunnel, my pack bouncing against my shoulder blades. Tormund jogged to catch up, then fell into step beside me in that sauntering walk of his.

"Don't you think it's important to sort this out?"

I cut my eyes his way. "By all means, stay and figure out what's going on with the sunstones."

A wry grin spread across his face. "Nice try, but you can't get rid of me that easily."

I heaved a sigh and stopped in the middle of the tunnel, throwing my arms wide. "Why, Tormund? Can't you just leave me to do my own thing? I know you're determined to find the Everstone, same as me, but I don't know where it is any more than you do. And it's not fair for you to dog my every step just to snatch it out from under my nose if I happen to stumble upon it. Go search another mine. *Alone.*"

He blinked, like he was shocked I'd actually stood up for myself. Bloomin' shadow demon.

"Well then. You're really saying how you feel, aren't you?" He had the nerve to look a bit hurt.

"I need to break my curse. I know you don't understand, but—"

"No, I do," he said quietly. "I understand far more than you think. And I want to offer you a deal."

I squinted at him. "What kind of deal?"

"One where we both get exactly what we want." Tormund closed the distance between us. His chest pressed against mine, and his eyes instantly went south. I didn't even attempt to cover up the hint of cleavage. If he wanted to get an eyeful, then he'd get an eyeful. Bet he liked what he saw, too. Good.

Wait a minute, I thought to myself. *Where in fate's name had that bloomin' thought come from!?!*

I stepped back, but I hit the stone wall, my head haloed by a cluster of dim sunstones. The dying glow glinted in the depths of Tormund's eyes, sparking something deep and aching inside me. Swallowing hard, I slid my finger beneath his chin and pushed it up. His gaze dragged back up to my face, but that wasn't any better. He looked like he was ready to *devour* me.

All the rumors I'd heard about shadow demons

echoed through my mind. They weren't known to be timid lovers. And when they chose a mate, they really *chose* one. They were raw and animalistic in their passions. At the thought of Tormund focusing all that intense energy on me, well. A blush was an understatement for how hot my face got.

"We both get what we want," I repeated, desperately trying to focus on the conversation rather than on the utter lack of space between our bodies. But then I struggled to think what Tormund wanted. Other than something raw and passionate. And if he wanted that with me, then I was afraid he'd be sorely disappointed with how that turned out.

I'd had a brief fling when I'd been much younger, but it hadn't lasted longer than a month, and I hadn't known what I was doing. Since then, I'd only shared a couple of kisses with one other. My experience in the romance department was… limited, to put it mildly.

"That's right," he said, his lips curling into a wicked smile. "Wouldn't you like that, Astrid?"

I nearly shuddered at the delicious way he spoke my name.

"That depends." I swallowed. "What is it that you want?"

"You know what I want," he said, practically purring now, strands of shadows curling and twisting around every inch of his body, including his deep black horns. The rhythm of their dance was mesmerizing, the way they whorled across his pale yet midnight-blue skin.

"Do I?" I whispered.

"The Everstone." His words snapped me out of my reverie. "Just like you."

"Right. The Everstone." I slid sideways. The rocky wall scraped my back, and then I found freedom in the open air, though a part of me ached to return to where I'd been—trapped with Tormund's body against mine, his shadows nearly engulfing us.

"What else would I be talking about?" he asked. "Is there something else on your mind?"

"No, Tormund." I sighed and rolled my eyes, desperately trying to cover up how flustered I'd gotten. "Just get on with it, all right? What's this deal you want to offer?"

His expression sobered. "We join forces to find the Everstone. The real one, wherever it is. You let me have it so I can return to Azraak and heal Tahir."

I scoffed. "That's not much of a deal. In fact, it's the *opposite* of a deal, because I get nothing out of it!"

"I will vow to find a way to undo your curse," he said solemnly. "And I do not take vows lightly.

In my eyes, they are unbreakable. My life will be dedicated to the cause. I swear it."

For a moment, I didn't know how to respond. I didn't much like his offer, mostly because I couldn't be sure if I could trust him. The only thing binding him to his promise was his integrity. He'd repeatedly made it clear he'd do anything to get his hands on that gem. Would he stoop so low to make a false vow?

My heart pounded my ribs. I wanted to believe him. I wanted to trust he was one of the good people of the world, that he wouldn't let me down. But it was a great bloomin' leap of faith.

I didn't need his help. I could find the stone on my own. And then I could un-curse myself.

And his brother would forever be trapped.

"Why can't it be the other way around?" I asked. "I could get the stone first, then we could search for another way to save your brother."

He rubbed the base of his horns, then sighed. "This is where I tell you I haven't been entirely truthful about Tahir."

"Wonderful." I folded my arms. "I should have known. Let me guess, you're not here for your brother, after all."

"I *am* here for Tahir," he said, his voice insistent. "But Tahir is not my brother. He's not even a shadow demon. He's a dragon, and the gem is the only thing that can heal the issue he has. A gem in Azraak caused it, so he needs a gem to undo it."

My hands fell to my sides. "A dragon?"

"I know." He took a step toward me. "It's hard to believe. Impossible, even. All the dragons were killed, right? Well, I'm here to tell you they weren't. One survived, and his name is Tahir."

"More than one survived," I told him.

"The talon you found? That doesn't belong to another dragon. All the dragons died, remember?" He sighed and ran his hands along his horns, shaking his head. "I believe someone has discovered why I'm here. They planted the talon as a warning of some kind. It explains all the other coincidences, too. Someone has it out for me."

"Hmm. Well, you might be right about the coincidences, but you're wrong about the dragon." I nibbled on my bottom lip, unsure if I should tell him. But he'd come clean to me, and if he was here to save a dragon, then I knew I could trust him with this information. "Four others have survived. They've lived in the Isles for well over a decade. And they're adolescents, growing rapidly every day, which means they want to spread their wings and explore. I think one of them came here for an adventure."

"Wait. You have four dragons on the Isles?" His

voice was flat, his eyes dark. For a moment, I wondered if I'd read him very, very wrong.

And then his entire face lit up. "Do you know what this means? Tahir won't be lonely anymore. Once I heal him, he can come here. He can soar through the clouds with his brethren."

17

ASTRID

Several hours later, Tormund and I perched on a rock overlooking a waterfall. Water rushed by us, swirling with froth, the sound filling the cave with a constant *shhhhhh*. I leaned back and pulled my knees to my chest, watching as he nibbled on a heel of bread, his eyes distant.

We had not come to an agreement on the deal. After we'd shared dragon stories, we'd started down the tunnel without question or comment, like we both knew we had to find this gem, one way or another.

My emotions warred for dominance. For as long as I could remember, I'd longed for freedom and to feel the warmth of the sun on my face. I'd learned of my curse when I'd been only two or three years old. Finding out was one of my first memories. I remembered Jostein sitting me down and explaining to me what it meant. Then he gave me a moss cake and a pat on the back, promising he'd always be there for me.

"But I want to go outside," I'd told him.

Smiling in that fatherly way of his, he'd replied, "Perhaps one day you will, but for now, you have all of us down here."

A couple of years later, I found the story of the Everstone in a book. That night, when I'd fallen asleep, I'd dreamt of getting my hands on the gem and sailing the salt sea with the beaming sun on my face.

Over the years, I'd grown more determined to find it. And to willingly walk away from it now felt like the unravelling of my soul. Everything I was and everything I'd planned to be—it all went back to the Everstone and my freedom. Who was I without it? What would I become?

I had nothing else, I realized. Nothing but my plants, which had taken over my home, and my mining job. Both of those were pretty great things, admittedly. I loved what I did, and tending to my plants and watching them thrive made *me* feel alive. And I had my friends, of course. This community in the dwarven mountains. I was never alone unless I wanted to be.

"You seem deep in thought," Tormund said,

nudging my knee with the back of his hand. His knuckles skimmed my trousers, but something about the intimacy of his touch made it feel like we were skin-to-skin.

"So do you," I pointed out. "What's on your mind?"

"The dragons," he said wistfully. "I'd love to see the sky full of wings."

"Yes. So would I."

"You will," he said. "We'll find the stone, I'll fix Tahir, and then we'll find a cure for you." He leaned forward, his arms resting on his thighs. From this position, he didn't tower over me like he usually did. We were eye to eye, and it was unnerving. "Think about it. This would save the species. Rivelin's dragons—the ones you told me about—are siblings. They'll never breed."

I nodded. "Lilia has mentioned that to me a time or two. She's beside herself since she's so attached to one of them. She hates the idea he's one of the last of his kind."

"He doesn't have to be," Tormund said quietly, his words nearly drowned out by the rush of the waterfall.

Tormund was right. Fates be damned, I hadn't thought of it that way before now, but there was no mistaking the truth in his words. If Tahir could leave his mountain, he could come here and ensure a future for dragons.

"What if we took Rivelin's dragons to Azraak instead?" I asked, offering the only other option I could think of.

Tormund shook his head. "I worry they'd succumb to the same affliction."

"Bloomin' fates," I muttered.

A slight smile lifted the corners of his lips. "Does that mean you'll agree to my deal?"

I nibbled on my bottom lip, then cursed again. "Yes, fine. I agree to your deal. But I need you to understand I'm doing this for the dragons, not you. I want a sky full of wings, too. After everything Isveig did to them, I want to see them thrive."

Tormund held out a hand, his eyes burning into mine. Shadows swirled around each of his fingers. Swallowing, I slid my palm into his. A searing heat whipped across my fingers, followed by the cooling touch of his shadows. I couldn't help but stare at them. They swirled around me, twisting up my arms and tracing circles against my skin, sensual and electric. And something about the way Tormund's hand held mine made it feel like a promise of things to come. Or an *invitation*.

I didn't know whether I wanted to lean in or pull away from him. And I didn't know what he would do in response to either one. And I certainly didn't know what I *wanted* him to do. What if I did give in to the sudden urge to lean closer? Would he wind his shadows further up my arm? Would he even go so far as to kiss me?

But what if I leapt to my feet and took off down the tunnel, resuming our search for the Everstone? Would he take that as a rejection of his invitation and never try again? Would I even *want* him to try again?

All these questions rattled around inside my brain like gemstones in a mine cart. I had two options, and I had no bloomin' idea which one I wanted, and I didn't want to choose for fear of chasing down the wrong thing.

So I did neither one.

I just sat there, staring into the depths of his midnight eyes, waiting for *him* to make the move.

Tension pounded between us. His shadows tightened around my arm. I pulled a breath into my lungs and held it there, my eyes darting down to his lips. And then, so slowly it was almost like it wasn't happening, he let his shadows fall from my skin.

Exhaling, he stood and rubbed the back of his neck. "I vow to find you a cure, Astrid. And I hope you know I'd sooner die than break a promise. You will step your feet on grassy land one day."

Disappointment flooded through me, rushing as

fast as the waterfall. I was so focused on his choice to pull away that I almost failed to register his promise. Oddly, it seemed to matter less in the moment. The gulf of cold air between us loomed so large.

"Thank you," I said crisply, then stood and brushed the dirt from my trousers.

Honestly, I'd been a fool to expect anything else, and I was even more of a fool to be disappointed by the lack of it. Other than his heated stares and his dancing shadows—which meant nothing from a shadow demon—he'd shown no interest in anything more than friendship. All right, sure, he'd flirted a little, too. But again, that meant nothing. He clearly had no interest in me.

And *I* had no interest in *him*, I reminded myself. Whatever I was feeling was only a result of his allure. Down here in the darkness of the mines, shadows were thick. It called at his allure and brought it to the surface. All of this was just magic and nothing more.

Besides, Tormund was only here for a short time. Soon, he would leave The Glass Peaks to return to Azraak. And as much as I yearned to breathe fresh air, walk barefoot through the grass, and bask in the morning sun's rays, I would never walk away from my home forever. I couldn't leave all this behind, and he might expect me to if we went further. Besides, there was no telling how long it would take to find my cure. I could be stuck here for years longer. Tormund would never want to be trapped in the dwarven mines.

I rolled my eyes at myself. What in fate's name was I even thinking? The demon hadn't even kissed me, let alone asked for a relationship. His allure really was a tricky bastard, wasn't it?

"Astrid?" Tormund asked with a frown.

"Yes, sorry." I'd been standing there far too long without speaking a word.

"You disappeared on me...everything all right?"

"I'm just thinking I hope we find this bloomin' dragon," I said. "We should get going."

He considered me for a moment, and I couldn't help but worry I'd never heard the full extent of shadow demon powers. What if they could read minds? Or infer thoughts based on facial expressions? Gods, he would know I'd been daydreaming about his bedroom eyes and contemplating how a relationship could work between us.

But then he stepped to the side and motioned me forward. "After you, Astrid."

My heart pounded. He really needed to stop saying my name like that.

We took off down the mine tunnels, following the fading light of the sunstones. The deeper we ventured, the darker it got. Tormund and I would not be discouraged, however. Our path continued ever forward, and we passed the time with lively conversation. He asked me about my life growing up, and I told him about Jostein and how he'd raised me as his own, training me young to work the mines. And then I asked about his childhood. The opposite of me, he had half a dozen siblings. They were all quite a bit older, and they'd left home a long time ago.

"I suppose they feel more like aunts and uncles than siblings," he told me. "And they're all scattered around the world now. I hardly ever see them."

"I'm sorry. That must be hard."

He shrugged, though I couldn't help but spot a flicker of pain in his eyes. "I've got Tahir. He's like a brother to me."

"Funny thing to say about a dragon," I replied with a smile.

"Once you meet him, you'll understand," said Tormund.

"Have you bonded with him?" I asked carefully. "I thought only orcs could do that."

Safely, anyway. Folk bonding with dragons had started the bloody war with Isveig—at least, that had been Isveig's excuse for destroying the dragons and conquering the orcs. Dragon magic was a volatile thing. Folk weren't meant to bond with that magic and channel it as their own. Only orcs could do it without losing control. More than one village had burned to a crisp because the wrong person had tried to bond with a dragon.

Eventually, folk stopped doing it. I thought we'd all learned our lesson. Bonding with dragons caused nothing but trouble.

I sent up a prayer to the gods that we weren't back there again.

"I wouldn't dream of it," Tormund said. "Tahir and I are brothers without needing a bond. I just can't go too near him. Otherwise, I risk getting burned. Just like anyone else who isn't an orc."

The heat that dragons emitted was far too powerful for most folk to withstand. We'd need to keep that in mind if we did find the creature we sought. If he were anywhere near the Everstone he'd stolen, we'd have to find some way to lure him away from it.

We came to the end of the path and ducked into another tunnel. The walls were low and narrow, and the sunstones were so few and far between now that I had to squint to see more than a few feet ahead. The scent of petrichor grew stronger, and the stones beneath our feet were slick, puddles forming from water trickling in through the walls.

"Why do you suppose he stole the gem, anyway?" I asked.

"Dragons treasure those who shine. And so do I." Tormund's voice was rough, and it dragged my attention away from my footsteps and to his face. He stared at me in the dim lighting, his eyes dark yet full of fire. Every part of me went hot with longing.

No one had ever looked at me that way.

"Tormund," I whispered.

He reached a hand toward my face, our footsteps in sync. My heart nearly pounded out of my chest. Whatever I'd felt before, I suddenly knew it hadn't been one-sided. There was something between us, against all odds. And even if it might end in nothing but pain, I was desperate to give in to it.

Tormund's thumb caressed my cheek. A sigh escaped my parted lips, and I started to lean into his touch.

But then the floor opened up beneath us, and we fell.

18

I shrieked as my bells filled the air with their song. The cavern walls rushed past me. I reached out to grasp at something—anything—but then my feet hit the ground. My teeth snapped shut; stars dotted my eyes. Shaking my head, I looked around. I hadn't fallen particularly far. If I were twice as tall, I might be able to reach the ledge above with a little jump.

"Tormund, I think you might be tall enough to reach that ledge. You could hoist me up on your shoulders, then follow me back up. What do you think?" I turned toward him, but...no one was there. Frowning, I tipped back my head. "Hallo! Looks like you missed the bloomin' hole! Lucky you! Mind helping me back up again?"

"I am afraid I did not miss the hole at all,"

called Tormund—from the opposite direction in which I looked.

"Oh no," I muttered, then looked down. Just to my left, the hole continued, opening up to an almost impenetrable darkness. Tormund's horns, cutting through the shadows, were the only thing I could see of him. And from the distance between me and him, it did not look like he could climb back out.

"I'm surprised you sound so worried," he said with forced laughter. "You're well and truly rid of me now."

"Are you all right?" I knelt beside the hole and peered into the depths. He'd fallen a lot further than I had.

"I'm fine. My shadows helped slow me. Too bad they couldn't stop me from falling in the first place."

"I'll get you out," I said matter-of-factly, dropping my pack. I rummaged around inside and pulled out a rope.

"You brought a rope with us?" he asked.

"Of course," I replied. "Dwarves never venture into the mines without proper supplies. The better question is, why didn't *you* bring one?"

"I didn't anticipate falling into a hole," he said flatly.

"Well, that was your first mistake. The second was not looking at where you were going."

"Very smug for the girl who *also* fell into a hole."

"I fell into the smaller hole, so I can be as smug as I bloomin' like, thank you very much." I grinned, unwinding the rope, the rough surface scratching my palms. Truth was, I had no idea how I would get him out of there, and joking seemed like the best way to keep both of us from panicking. Sure, I could toss him the end of the rope. It was plenty long enough to reach him. Just like I'd told him, us dwarves liked to be prepared. The problem was, he was twice as big as I was. How would I find the strength to pull him out?

So before I could talk myself out of it, I tossed one end of the rope into the hole. It hit the ground only a second later, and I felt a tug as Tormund tested the weight of it.

"There's a stone beside you," he called out. "You could tie it around that."

I frowned at said stone. I'd noticed it before but hadn't considered it an option. Like us, it had fallen here some time ago and only came to my hips.

"It's loose," I told him. "And I don't think it's large enough to hold your weight. I'm afraid it will slide into the hole and fall on your head if you try it. You'll turn into a smashed demon."

"That's a mental image I could have done without," he said, his laughter tense. Then his laughter died. "Wait a moment."

"What is it?" Frowning, I peered over the side of the hole, but I could see nothing but darkness.

"Forget about saving me. You need to come down here and see this," he said, his voice now sounding a little further away.

"You want me to jump in there with you? Have you lost your bloomin' mind? We'll never get out of here if I do that."

He chuckled. "No jumping. Just climb down the rope. You're lighter than me. I'm sure the stone will hold your weight. And if it doesn't, I'll catch you."

I squinted down into the darkness. "This sounds like a terrible idea."

"Which part?"

"All of it."

He laughed, the sound echoing all around me. A smile quirked my lips, and I shook my head. "Only you'd find this funny. You do know these tunnels are so far from the mines that it'll be a long time before anyone comes through here."

"Just come down, Astrid. I promise you'll be happy you did," he said in a deep voice that seemed to curl around me and beckon me toward the hole.

"Did you just use your shadow demon powers

on me?" I asked, tossing my end of the rope around the stone and tying a dwarven knot.

"It worked, didn't it?"

"No, I'm only doing this because my curiosity won't let me do anything else. I want to see what's gotten you so excited."

"There's quite a few things in these tunnels that's gotten me excited."

I shook my head, finished tying the knot, and threw him a *look*. I might not be able to see him, but I knew he could see me. "Are you just constantly waiting for someone to say something that you can turn around and make a suggestive joke about?"

"No." A pause. "But I do look for any opportunity to make you smile."

Heat burned my chest, right around my heart. I knew it was probably just another one of his jokes—a way to keep us both distracted from the fact we were stuck here without any help coming our way. And I would just have to keep joking right back.

"Well, I hate to disappoint you, but your remarks aren't particularly funny," I said, sticking my tongue out at him.

"Could have fooled me," he said, his voice growing quiet. "Your eyes do this thing when you smile—genuinely smile. I wish you could see how happy you are when you're not focused on trying to escape the mountain."

My hands fell to my sides. "I know I'm happy here. This is my home."

"Then why are you trying so hard to leave?"

"I..." My thoughts evaded me. I shook my head, trying to recall the reasons I'd repeated in my head all these years. I wanted to see the sun and the grass and the trees. There was so much life outside the mountain. But there was so much inside it, too. "I don't know. I just want to see what's out there."

"I can tell you what's out there. A big, beautiful world," he said.

"All right." My brow furrowed. "I'm not sure what your point is, Tormund. You tell me I'm happy in Steingard and you don't understand why I want to leave, but then you say how beautiful the world is."

"That's because it is. The whole bloomin' thing, as you'd say. It's also a big old place with lands far, far from these shores. One could spend her whole life exploring, and she'd never see it all. Not every corner, every person, every creature. There would always be something just out of reach."

I pressed my lips together. I saw where he was going with this now.

"You're already trying to back out of our deal," I said flatly.

"No, I'm not. It's just..." He sighed.

"Just what?" I demanded.

"You won't like it."

I narrowed my eyes, wishing I could see his face, if only so I could properly glare at him. "Just tell me, Tormund."

A beat passed. "There will be a reason you were cursed and a fairly simple way to undo it."

A hectic drumming sounded in my ears, and after a moment, I realized it was the thunder of my beating heart. An eerie chill swept through the cavern, lingering on the back of my neck like icy fingers. Tormund's words seemed to cut to my very bones. They made me want to leave him in the pit and flee from this place, though I had no idea why they'd caused this kind of reaction.

"I don't understand what you're saying," I eventually said. "I was *you know* as a babe. I did nothing to cause this."

"Curses don't happen for no reason, Astrid. Whoever did it did so for a reason, especially if you were so young you can't even remember it."

I threw up my hands. "Perhaps I cried too loudly, I don't know. Maybe someone got annoyed by all the noise and wanted to punish me."

"It could be that, I'll admit," said Tormund. "But often, there's some kind of lesson involved. Learn it. Accept it. And I bet your curse will break."

"Let me guess. You think I should stop wanting to go outside."

"You said it. Not me," came the reply.

I was starting to get tired of having a conversation with a pit of darkness. Sighing, I wrapped my hands around the rope and eased back. The emptiness yawned beneath me, beckoning me to leap into its less-than-gentle embrace. Tormund had said he'd catch me if I fell, but what if the boulder rolled in after me, like I'd worried it would do to him?

"You've got this, Astrid. Easily. Believe in your damn self for once," he called up.

He was right. I could do this. Without letting my thoughts talk me out of it, I pushed off the ledge. The ground opened up beneath me. I swung to the left, my feet dangling. Then I twisted the rope between my thighs and began my descent. Hand over hand, I went down. Only seconds later, my feet made contact with the ground, and all the tension flooded from my body. That had been easy. What had I been so worried about?

"See?" Tormund appeared before me, beaming. "You're incredible."

I flushed. "Thank you."

"You can do anything you put your mind to," he murmured.

"Like leave this mountain?"

"You don't like what I said. I thought that might be the case." He rubbed the base of his horns, then sighed. "It would make things so much simpler for you if you understood what I'm trying to tell you, but I suppose that's the entire point. If it were easy, it wouldn't be a curse. No matter. We'll find another way."

"If what you're saying is true, it probably wouldn't even work now. To give up on going outside so that I can then go outside is kind of the opposite of what needs to happen. I would actually have to give up."

"Ah, but there you're wrong." He tapped me on the nose. "It's not giving up anything. It's embracing what you have. Now, come on."

He took off across the cavern. The low cave stretched far in every direction, and over a dozen tunnels forked off from this area. Water gushed from a large crack, pouring into a river that snaked through the room toward a pond. The scent of ash overwhelmed the moss and stone, tempting my attention toward a low crack in the wall, barely large enough for one person if they were on their belly in a crawl. A glowing ember light spilled from it, flashing dancing shadows on the wall.

I pointed at said crack. "There's a dragon through there, isn't there?"

"That or someone has made themselves a camp in the middle of this cave system. Which I suppose is possible, though highly unlikely."

"All right." I squared my shoulders. "Let's go."

"Astrid, wait." Tormund grabbed my hand, stopping me before I got more than a few steps away from him. He pulled me back and tugged me up against him. My hands squashed between my breasts and his chest because I had no idea what else to do with them. I couldn't very well *wrap them around his waist,* now could I?

"What is it?" My words came out in a whisper.

"This could be dangerous. I don't know if we should go in there without knowing what we'll find."

Right. That was what this was about. Safety. Not kissing me.

I pulled out of his arms. "It's just an adolescent dragon. One of Rivelin's, probably. And his dragons are friendly."

"What if it's not one of his? What if it's something else?"

"What else could it be?" I shook my head at him. He'd been so determined to come down here, I hadn't expected this sudden uncertainty.

"It's just…" He frowned. "I still feel like something isn't quite right about all of this. If the dragon and the Everstone are through that tunnel, then didn't we find it a little too easily?"

I squinted at him. "I'm not sure 'easy' is the word I would use for falling into a hole."

"But isn't it odd we didn't see the hole?"

Heart constricting, I looked everywhere but at his face. Was he really going to make me say it out loud? So far, neither one of us had commented on the moments leading up to our disaster. We'd simply fallen into a hole that had come out of nowhere! It had nothing to do with the fact we were both staring at each other so intently that we'd missed the very obvious lack of floor.

"*Was* it odd, though?" I asked, the pitch of my voice going higher. "We were kind of, well, distracted. If you don't remember."

Did he remember? Or had I simply imagined the entire thing?

But then he stepped in close, gripped my chin between his fingers, and tilted back my head. "Speaking of distractions, I still haven't done this."

19

ASTRID

Tormund angled his head, and my hands tumbled to my sides. Gently, he pressed his lips against mine. Warmth flooded my senses. With a satisfied growl, he deepened the kiss and parted my lips with his tongue. I reached up and clutched his shoulders and closed my eyes, the tension in my body keeping me as tight as a rod.

His hand snaked down my side and rested on my hip. I leaned into his chest, tasting him, feeling him, revelling in the way his body seemed to hum. Shadowy strands encircled every spot we touched, pulsing in time with the frantic beat of my heart, like they could feel the intoxicating thrill coursing through my body.

He continued to kiss me. His mouth against

mine was electric, but there was a gentleness in the way he touched me, like I was made of glass, and he was afraid I might shatter if he pushed too hard. The ache within me deepened, burning up a hole in my core. And when he moved his lips to my neck, I felt like I might very well combust.

I'd thought of this more times than I wanted to admit. How would he taste? Like chocolate, it turned out. How would he feel? Strong and powerful, like he could toss me onto a bed and put me exactly where he wanted me. How would he sound? The low rumble of his chest suggested he was enjoying this as much as I was—if not more.

I curled my fingers tighter around his tunic, pushed up onto my toes, and kissed him—*really* kissed him.

This wasn't shadow demon magic. It wasn't an allure or some kind of tempting trick. This feeling came straight from the heart of me. I wanted Tormund. It didn't matter that we could have no future together. All that mattered was right here and now. He would be around for at least a week or two longer, and we could make the most of it.

But then suddenly, he released me, stepped back, and ran his fingers through his hair. His face almost looked pained.

My stomach dropped. Dread crept along the back of my neck. Had I gotten this all wrong? Had I read too much into this kiss? Was it...*was it* the shadow magic, after all?

Gods, how mortifying if it was.

"I'm sorry," he said, his voice still a growl, though laced with what sounded like regret. "I got carried away."

I clenched my teeth. All the visions of us spending the next ten days together puffed away like his silken shadows. It'd been a silly little dream. And he'd encouraged it. He never should have kissed me if he hadn't meant it.

If kissing me was getting *carried away*.

"It's fine. Don't make the same mistake again," I said tightly.

Without another glance in his direction, I ducked and slid into the tunnel. Tormund loosed a grunt, but I ignored him. I crawled forward against the wet stone ground, the orange glow flickering at the other end of the tunnel. From here, I could more clearly see what lay beyond. A cavern large enough to hold an entire dwarven village widened before me, and the floor transformed into rolling hills of gold coins. Sunstones were scattered amongst them, as well as powerless gemstones of every color imaginable. Throughout it all sat treasure trunks packed with trinkets, the lids cast open or torn from their hinges. Even a few mine carts had been consumed by the avalanche of gold.

But there was one thing that stood out from the rest. A dragon with flaming orange scales curled around it all, clutching some of the sunstones into her wings. Her ridged back rose and fell in a steady rhythm, and her eyes were closed, so she did not spot the dwarven woman crawling into her lair.

I pulled a breath into my lungs and held it there. For the first time in my life, I'd set my eyes on a dragon. She was a magnificent, gorgeous creature, her long talons glinting against the sunstones' steady glow. Small horns decorated her snout, trailing to more on the back of her head that were almost as tall as I was. Every wing was tipped with them, too.

And those membranous wings suddenly twitched.

I stilled, my heart in my throat. While she clearly wasn't fully grown, she was still incredibly large—especially compared to me. She could chomp me to bits if she wanted to, and that was if she didn't use her internal fires to burn me alive for daring to step on her gold.

Tormund slithered up beside me, his horns scraping the low ceiling. He kept his eyes on the dragon rather than take a chance by looking at me. After a moment, he let out a tense breath.

Leaning closer, he pressed his lips against my ear. "Is that one of his?"

His being Rivelin's, I could only assume.

I shrugged as best I could in the cramped conditions. While Lilia had told me many stories about Rivelin and his dragons, I'd never seen them. Rivelin had never wanted to leave Hearthaven to visit The Glass Peaks, and so his dragons had never ventured this far from home. Until now, at least.

Although if this dragon's hoard was any indication, she'd been here a while.

If she wasn't one of Rivelin's dragons, my questions were endless. First—and most importantly—why did it look like there were some chocolate bars in one of the open trunks? But second, was she friendly? If I climbed out of this little crack in the wall, would she roast me, or would she listen to what I had to say?

Tormund's thoughts seemed to follow a similar pattern. Maybe minus the chocolate. He tugged on my sleeve and jerked his chin in the direction we'd come. He wanted to get out of there.

No, thank you.

He'd been encouraging me to believe in myself. Well, now was the time to put his advice into practice. I grinned and patted his arm—awkwardly so, what with how we were crawling around on our bellies. Then I shoved myself forward, out of the tunnel, and right onto a very hard and pointy bed of gold coins.

They jingled a jaunty little tune, blending with the sound of my bells. I froze and held my breath, palms slick against the coins. The dragon didn't flinch. She continued to sleep, her nostrils flaring with every breath. My fingers itched to rip the bells from my hair. I wore them so often, I'd sort of forgotten I'd left them there. And now it was too late to do a damn thing about them.

Tormund emphatically waved at me from the tunnel. Ignoring him, I pushed onto my knees and released my hand from the ground. A few gold coins stuck to my palms, then fell. One by one.

Clink.

Clink.

CLIIIIIIINK.

I squeezed my eyes tight and braced myself for a fiery impact.

None came.

Biting the insides of my cheeks, I squinted open a single eye, like that would be safer than opening both of them. Still, the dragon slept.

I craned my head over my shoulder, shuddering from the impact of my heart against my ribs. Tormund's face was grim. He crawled forward, emerging from the tunnel. I shook my head at him, motioning for him to return to the shadows. I was much smaller than him, and my hair was similar enough to the color of the sunstones. I might not stand out amongst her trea-sures if I remained still when the dragon opened her eyes.

Tormund, however, was unmissable. His shadows seemed to swallow up all the surrounding light, and his pale, midnight-blue skin was a stark contrast to the gold of the coins. But instead of ducking back into the safety of the tunnel, he moved toward me. His heavy boots hit the treasure mountain, and the coins rushed sideways, tumbling over each other in a waterfall of gold.

I clenched my teeth, shooting daggers with my eyes. I swore to the gods, if he got himself eaten by a dragon, then I'd...well, I'd find a way to bring him back to life so I could remind him just how monstrously large his ego was for coming in here like this.

I can handle this on my own!

I tried to send him that message with my eyes, but he was too focused on the dragon to notice—or too busy avoiding my gaze after the whole kiss thing. Maybe both.

I folded my arms. How utterly unsurprising. Not only had he immediately regretted our kiss, but now he couldn't meet my eyes. When I continued shooting daggers—sharper this time— and he continued to avoid me, I loosed an exasper-ated sigh and elbowed him.

"Astrid," he said in a whisper, "is now *really* the time for this?"

"The time for what?" I hissed. "To talk about why you kissed me when you clearly didn't want to?"

"I *did* want to," he mouthed.

I rolled my eyes. "Right. Of course. And now you don't want to, so you're ignoring me even though *I am standing right next to you inside a dragon's lair.*"

"I did try to stop you from coming in here, if you remember."

"Oh, I remember everything," I said bitterly. "The way you looked at me, the way you used your stupid shadow demon allure against me, and the way you turned it all off out of nowhere."

"Astrid." His eyes slid my way then. Regret and pain flared in their shadows. "You don't want to get involved with me. Trust me. I'm sorry I got so carried away. You're just...so damn beautiful I forgot myself." He sighed and turned back to the dragon. "It won't happen again."

"You don't get to tell me what I do or don't want."

"Astrid."

"No." I took a step toward him, no longer caring about the clatter of the gold coins. "You can tell me you don't want me or that you didn't enjoy our kiss, though I know that'd be a lie. But what you *can't* do is decide what I want."

"Astrid, keep looking at me. The dragon is awake now."

My eyes nearly bugged out of my head. "Oh."

"We might want to back away." His voice was shockingly calm, though his jaw clenched from the tension. Tormund held up his hand and flicked his fingers behind him. My mouth went dry. He wanted me to go first.

"Is she looking in our direction?" I whispered, trying to remain as still as possible. If she hadn't spotted us yet, I didn't want to help her find us.

A grim smile spread across Tormund's face. "You might say that."

Bloomin' fates. Shoulders tensing, I swung my gaze toward the dragon. She'd unfurled from her perch on the top of the gold coin mountain, her nostrils flared. Two ember eyes started right at me and Tormund. Fire licked her bared teeth, sharper than any blade.

Terror tumbled through my churning stomach. "Uh oh."

"Go, Astrid. If you're quick, you can get out of here alive," he said, his mouth barely moving.

"You know, she can probably hear what you're saying just fine," I said. "No need to mumble anymore."

As if in answer to my statement, the dragon lifted her head from the gold and swung her snout in our direction. Flames licked the coins surrounding her talons, and the stench of char flared through the cavern, consuming us whole.

20

TORMUND

When the dragon breathed its fire, I threw myself in front of Astrid. I spread my arms wide and flung out my shadows, bracing myself for the pain of flesh melting from my bones. Heat stormed toward me and curled against my face, but then the cool touch of my shadows shoved it away.

My shoulder hit the coins hard. The clatter of my teeth rang through my skull, nearly drowning out Astrid's cry of alarm. My stomach dropped. The distinct lack of furious pain told me I'd survived just fine. Which meant I'd failed. I hadn't been fast enough to stop the flames from claiming Astrid.

Gods, I have to get her out of here.

I rolled over and leapt to my feet, my heart

thundering so hard I could barely breathe. Astrid stood just behind me with a shaking hand pressed to her mouth. Her face was stark white, but she was *fine*. But fear painted every feature.

Her knees buckled. I shot out an arm, catching her waist just before she fell.

"Whoa, there," I said, tucking my other arm beneath her legs and hauling her up against my chest. Her eyes had slid shut, but she was still breathing.

"I'm fine," she said in barely a whisper. "I just got light-headed is all."

Still, worry wormed its way through my gut, and all I could think of was a dumb joke. "Keep this up, and I'll lose count of how many times my handsome charm has made you faint."

She let out a breathy chuckle. "There's that ego. I was starting to miss it."

Something unsettling tightened in my stomach, and I had to admit that Astrid Balstad had well and truly gotten under my skin. I'd been desperate to kiss her earlier, landing us both in a heap of trouble.

I could not get involved with her more than I already had. The last thing I wanted to do was hurt her, and I would. Nothing good could come from this. I had to stop seeing her.

But I would get her back home safely first.

I held her tighter against my chest. "You're all right? None of the fire got you?"

She cracked open her eyes. "She didn't actually breathe any on us."

I glanced over my shoulder. The dragon had returned to her perch, talons curled protectively around a trunk that held a dizzying amount of chocolate bars. "Right. Well, it looked like she was going to."

Astrid grinned up at me, the corners of her eyes crinkling. "You leapt in front of me, Tormund."

Clearing my throat, I shifted on my feet. "I fell."

"No, you jumped in front of me to take the brunt of the fire," she said insistently. "You tried to save my life."

"You make it sound far more noble than it was. Anyone else would have done the same thing."

"That is absolutely untrue. Most people would run screaming. But you didn't. You tried to save my life." A pause, and then her voice went soft. "Thank you."

I couldn't help it. My chest puffed up a bit, and my arms instinctively tightened around her body, where I still held her against me. "All right, let's not make a fuss of it."

And then the most delightful sound in the world met my ears. Astrid *giggled*. It was a different laughter than any I'd heard from her before. Those had always been chuckles or laughs, but *this*. There was something so light-hearted and free about it, as if the chains that burdened her had finally broken off. Warmth curled through me, and for a moment, it was hard to remember why I was so determined to keep my distance.

"You? Not making a fuss of yourself?" She giggled again. "Maybe I need to be the one holding *you* up because I think you're feeling quite funny in the head right now, Mr. Tormund Bakke, the big, bad shadow demon who is good at everything."

"Good at everything, eh?" I cocked a brow, grinning.

"Ah, there he is again." Beaming, she tapped my nose. "Can you put me down now? I think the dragon wants us to leave."

As loathe as I was to let go, I lowered Astrid onto the pile of gold coins. We turned toward the dragon in unison. She watched us through half-lidded eyes, her tail twitching against the coins.

"I think that is an annoyed twitch," I said.

"Very observant of you," Astrid quipped.

I sighed, relaxing. But deep down, I knew this bone-deep relief had nothing to do with the dragon's lack of fire and everything to do with Astrid's improved mood. My reaction to the kiss had hurt her, and I couldn't stand it.

"You don't think we should try talking to her?

After all this effort, I hate to leave without the Everstone."

She cocked her head, considering the dragon. "Do you see anything that looks like the gem?"

"I was hoping you did," I said.

There were plenty of sunstones—enough to light every dwarven home for miles. Other gems littered the gold, but most were common ones, like rubies and onyx, none of which had magical properties. Pretty, yes, but sparkly things would do nothing but gain us some coin. And I wasn't about to try stealing from a dragon to line my pockets. She hadn't doused us in fire, but I was fairly certain she would if we took anything.

"Maybe she's lying on top of it," Astrid tried.

"She's not in the same spot as she was in before. I would have noticed it."

"Bloomin' fates," Astrid muttered. "You think she hid it somewhere in all this gold? I don't suppose she'd let us start digging through it...right?"

"Unlikely. Besides, I doubt she'd bury the best prize." I looked at Astrid and smiled. "She'd want it where she could enjoy it anytime she liked."

She cut her eyes my way. "Is that another innuendo?"

Yes, but not in the way you think.

I'd been thinking about her laugh and her smile.

Nothing about her glorious hips and the treasure that would lay between her thighs. But *now* I was thinking about both those things and more. And I could tell by the sudden spark in her eyes that her mind had gone in a very similar direction. I wondered what she thought of my horns. I'd imagined—on more than one occasion—how it would feel to have her hold on to them while I trapped her against the wall and followed through on all my innuendos. There wasn't a single doubt in my mind she'd feel as good as she looked.

Instead of saying all that, I winked.

Her face flushed. "You're completely hopeless." A pause. "So what do we do now?"

What I wanted to do was, unfortunately, not in the current realm of possibility. We were inside a dragon lair, and I didn't want to suck Astrid into my doomed world. Both of those thoughts kept me focused on the task at hand rather than the way her tunic hugged her breasts in a way that outlined every curve.

I cleared my throat. "I think we leave the dragon alone for now. Are there any other tunnels we could search before returning to Steingard?"

She pursed her luscious lips, then nodded. "There are miles of tunnels. We could spend months searching them all."

"I'm willing to do that if you are," I said, then

mentally kicked myself. Did I really want to suggest spending the next several months travelling through these mines, just the two of us? I'd likely manage to keep my hands to myself for precisely one night.

"What, *now*?" She tugged on a strand of hair, and her bells rang. "We'd need far more supplies. A real tent. Lots of food. Maybe some chocolate bars, if we could find some. For energy purposes, of course."

I quirked a smile. "Of course. We can return to Steingard first and spend a few days getting things together."

She cocked her head. "You're serious about this."

"Astrid Balstad, I travelled here all the way from Azraak just to find the Everstone. I'm not leaving until I find it. And if that means seeing every inch of these dwarven mines, then so be it."

And if it means spending all that time with you, even better.

"What about the Fittest Under the Mountain competition?" she asked. "We both entered it. Thor won't let us walk away."

"Luckily, I don't think Jostein will restart the trials until the Everstone is found."

Astrid shook her head and glanced at the dragon, who'd closed her eyes and drifted back to sleep. That or she was lying in wait to see if we'd attempt to steal anything from her. A look of disappointment crossed Astrid's face. She'd truly believed the dragon had stolen the treasure, and I'd hoped for the same. Deep down, I'd doubted it, though.

Nothing about this sat right with me. And I would not stop searching until I found the answers.

Eventually, Astrid nodded. "All right. Let's do this. You and me, travelling through the mines." Then she giggled. My gut twisted again. That beautiful, musical sound. "Hopefully, we don't end up driving each other mad."

And hopefully, I wouldn't fall in love with her by the end of it.

21

ASTRID

The route back to Steingard was long and arduous. I managed to scale the rope to the first hole's ledge, then use my weight, combined with the rock, to help Tormund follow. We wound up back in the tunnel where we'd been too busy staring at each other to notice the massive hole in the ground. It turned out that tunnel was a dead end, anyway, so we would have had to turn around and go back if we hadn't explored the holes.

Tormund spent a long time frowning at the dead end before trailing after me in the direction from whence we came. My limbs felt as heavy as my eyelids, and my mind was too frazzled to conjure thoughts. We were far enough away from the Endless Chasm that we wouldn't hear the dwarven bell that signalled sundown. I had no idea what time it was or how long I'd been awake. Judging by my staggering exhaustion, it was well past my bedtime.

Still, we carried on, shuffling down tunnel after tunnel—until finally, we walked out into the fresh breeze rolling through the Endless Chasm, the scent of daises wafting toward us. I squinted, trying to make out where we were, but shadows clung to every ledge, transforming the whole place into nothing more than stone smudges.

"Hmm," Tormund said from beside me. "I haven't been here long, but something tells me there's something very wrong with your sunstones."

I hadn't registered it until he said it. We'd spent so many hours in the darkness of the lower mines that the heavy shadows here seemed normal. But every sunstone along the many ledges lining the chasm was almost completely dark. All the bridges were dark, too. A tremor went down my spine. No one was out here replacing the stones, either, as far as I could tell.

It was so quiet that I could hear the distant trickle of cave water trailing down the walls.

"We can't live like this. Someone has to do something," I said quietly, resignation settling in my gut. "I can't go with you, Tormund. I need to help with the mining efforts. We need more sunstones to replace all these."

"Astrid." He settled a warm, comforting hand on my shoulder. "I think we both know that's not going to help."

I closed my eyes, an uneasy breath rattling through me. Things had been off when we'd left. The sunstones at The Wet Beard had been fading. The ones along the bridge near my home had been, too. Even those we'd passed in the mines had seemed dimmer than usual, but I'd been so focused on our quest that I'd banished the problem from my mind.

Now the truth was impossible to ignore.

Something was very, very wrong with our sunstones.

"Come on." I tugged on his arm, letting my instincts lead the way. Without the sunstones, we had no light, no warmth, and no way to grow food. Our entire society depended on these gems, and if we didn't find a way to fix whatever was wrong with them, the dwarves would have to find another home.

The idea of it burned the back of my throat. The dwarves had lived here for so long. I couldn't imagine where else we could go.

The Wet Beard was dark and cold. No one sat at the tables. The bard stage was empty. Empty tankards lined the bar, and no one was in the back office. They'd cleaned up the smashed crate and washed the walls, but the scent of smoke still lingered. Tormund and I looked around for a while, then moved on to the arena where the first trial had been held.

Not a single soul stirred in the expansive space or the circular stands.

"This is eerie," I whispered. My quiet voice bounced along the vaulted ceiling. Dust motes danced in the dim light filtering through the small cracks far above. It was the only light I'd seen since leaving the tunnels.

"Everyone's likely taken refuge in their homes," Tormund answered. "Many will be frightened."

"They are," a deep voice called out from behind us.

I turned to find Jostein emerging from the shadows, his gray brow slamming low over his eyes. He walked slowly as if the simple act was almost too exhausting to bear. My heart beat painfully against my ribs. I could only imagine how rough the past day must have been, with all the lights blinking out. Jostein would have tried to make order out of chaos and field questions to which he did not know the answers.

"What's happening, Jostein?" I asked him.

He slowed to a stop, sighed, and tugged at his long beard. "Truth be told, Astrid, I have no idea. The sunstones have stopped working. Even the ones we've yet to mine. We can't replace any of the faded ones because there's none to replace them with. I don't understand why this has happened or how to fix it."

"I have an idea," I said grimly. The thought had been rattling around in my brain all the way from The Wet Beard to the arena. The sunstones had never failed us before. They'd burned brightly for so very long. There was no reason they should suddenly fade like this. Not unless something had changed.

And something very big *had* changed. Only one thing had, really.

The only problem was, I didn't want to be right about this. Because it meant both the end of Tormund's dream and mine.

Jostein arched his brow, waiting for my thought.

"It's the Everstone," I admitted. "I think removing it from the tunnels has caused this. It must be what powers the sunstones and has kept our community thriving the way it has. And if we don't find it and put it back where it came from, well…then I think life as we know it is over. We'll have to move on to somewhere else."

I looked up at Tormund. He nodded, his lips set into a thin line. He'd come to the same conclusion I had.

"Ah, yes." Jostein shuffled his feet a bit. "About that. The, ah, Everstone prize isn't really the Everstone."

Tormund swore. "I bloody knew it."

Jostein gave him a look. "The one you saw *is* a powerful gemstone, but it's not *the* Everstone."

"What do you mean?" I asked with a frown.

He heaved a sigh. "Rockheim wanted the Everstone. They traded their emerald one for it. I didn't think it really mattered. This new gem is powerful enough. What do we need the Everstone for?"

"To power our whole bloomin' community, Jostein!" I shouted, my voice echoing through the arena. "You just gave away the source of our light, our heat, and the only way we're able to grow food down here in The Deep. Can that new gemstone do any of that? What's its power, anyway?"

Paling, he stared down at his feet. "I thought it was fairly impressive, Astrid. It can give its bearer endless gold."

My stomach bottomed out. The dragon and her lair. "Endless *gold coins*, perhaps?"

He lifted his eyes. "Yes, I suppose. If that's the form one wished it to take. A truly great prize for winning the Fittest Under the Mountain, don't you think?"

"Well, everything makes a lot more sense." Throwing up my hands, I walked away. I knew Jostein had meant well. To him, the gem was just a gem. He hadn't known the consequences of removing it from our world. And in his eyes, endless gold in the hands of one of our own was probably a good thing, as long as they weren't a greedy bastard like Galinn. And as I thought back to the first trial, I recognized Jostein had been all too willing to remove him from the competition when given the chance. He'd wanted someone else to win. Maybe even me.

Still, none of that changed the facts. The Everstone was gone. And if we didn't get it back, the light would be gone forever.

Tormund rested his hand on my shoulder. I looked up into the concerned eyes of the only person in the world I wanted to see right now, strangely enough. He'd understand how I felt more than anyone else. He knew how important this was.

"Are you all right?" he murmured.

"I'm really bloomin' angry."

"Understandable. He gave away the one thing he knew could set you free."

"No, it's not about that." I shook my head, my bells jingling. "He should have talked to me about the Everstone, but not because of that. Giving it away was a big decision, and he made it all on his own. I know he's the one who runs our community, not me. But…I'm just shocked he would hide something like that from me. From all of us."

"I don't want to defend him. He did a dumb thing. But he can't have known the damage it would cause the sunstones," he said. "That said, I fully support whatever you want to do. If you want to throw something at him, I'll hand you a rock." He grinned. "I hope you've been practicing your aim."

I giggled. I couldn't help myself. The tension and worry and anxiety of the past few days were finally catching up to me, and I sorely needed a release. And right now, Tormund and his dumb jokes felt the perfect source of that.

"Ah, that's a nice sound to hear." He tweaked my chin, winking at me. "Should I make another innuendo to keep it going?"

My chest warmed. "I actually wouldn't say no to that." Then I sighed. "I suppose it's time to go home and start packing up my things, what little of it there is."

He looked at me for a long moment, then asked, "Why would you go and do a thing like that?"

"The Everstone is gone. The northern dwarves will have to move. To where, I don't know, but we can't stay here. I suppose some of us will go up top. Others will head south to Rockheim. Maybe that's where I'll go, too. They're the ones with the Everstone, after all. I bet their sunstones work just fine."

"Everyone will be staying right where they are." He held out a hand, palm up. "You and I are going to fix this."

"How?" I slid my hand into his and nearly sighed in contentment when his warmth pressed against my skin.

"Simple. We go to Rockheim, and we tell them what's happened. As long as they're good people, they'll let you have the Everstone back."

"Oh." I smiled. "That's actually not a terrible idea."

Jostein cleared his throat. "Ah, about that. You might have a small problem if you go to them empty-handed."

Tormund lifted his head and gave Jostein a look so brutally harsh that I could have clapped. "Do explain."

Jostein shuffled uneasily. "We signed a contract during the trade. If we want to undo the exchange, the gem or something of the same value must be offered. Essentially, they'll need their gem back for us to get ours."

"And that's despite the fact our community will cease to exist without the Everstone?" I asked, my heart pounding.

"The contract was written in blood. It cannot be undone, even if they agree to it."

Tormund swore.

"Right. Thank you, Jostein, for this impossible task." Sighing, I squared my shoulders and patted down my hair. "It doesn't matter. I know exactly how to fix this. It's simple. I have to bribe a dragon."

22

ASTRID

Lilia, Ragnar, Daella, and Rivelin were nowhere to be found. They knew all about dragons. In fact, the one lurking in the mine tunnels was likely one of Rivelin's friends. And if not, Daella was an orc who could approach the beast without getting burnt. We needed their help. Desperately. But after searching every tavern in the area, I came up empty. It seemed they'd either left the mountains or gone searching the mine tunnels on their own.

"It couldn't be easy, could it?" I pulled a stool up to a table at The Wet Beard and pointed for Tormund to sit. No one was here to serve us ale, but that didn't mean we couldn't enjoy it.

Right now, I sorely needed to take the edge off with a delicious brew.

As I grabbed a keg and poured the drinks, Tormund leaned against the counter, far more at ease than he had any right to be. Didn't he understand the implications of this? He seemed content to let me find the Everstone and return it to its rightful place, but that meant he couldn't take it back to Azraak to save his friend.

"We've been to see the dragon once already. We'll figure it out," he said.

I pushed a tankard across the counter, then took a big gulp of mine. I downed the whole thing at once, slammed it onto the bar, and poured another.

His eyebrow arched skyward. "Thirsty?"

"You seem awfully calm." I took another drink —this time just one sip instead of the entire brew— and met his stare with one of my own. "I need you to answer a question, and I need you to answer it honestly."

"What is it, Astrid?"

I tried not to shudder at the way he said my name. Gods, why did it always get to me like that?

"Once we found out where the gem went, you instantly relaxed. It's like you believe there's no reason to worry. You don't seem disappointed that you must give it up for the dwarves to survive here. Tell me the truth, Tormund. Are you going to take the gem back to Azraak?"

He leaned forward and gazed at me with an intensity that made my toes curl. "No."

"Really," I said. Not a question, a statement. "You're not going to take the Everstone home?"

"There are thousands of you. I'd never take away the one thing that means you can survive in your mountain."

"But your dragon friend…"

He sighed. "I'll find another way."

"You said there was no other way," I argued.

"I said it needed to be a gemstone. Perhaps there's another that can do what must be done. Tahir can survive in the mountains until I find another way. Your villages and cities can't."

I blew out a breath. If it hadn't been for his reaction to our first kiss, I could have launched myself at him. He'd willingly give the dwarves the one thing he wanted most in the world, and he didn't even seem upset about it. He hadn't complained as he'd helped me search for Lilia and Rivelin these past few hours. He'd been there every step of the way, encouraging me with concern written in every inch of his eyes.

"Thank you," I said, almost breathlessly.

"Do you know what I noticed, Astrid?" he asked.

"What's that?"

He quirked a smile. "You haven't mentioned your own damn self once."

"I...what do you mean?" I felt the urge to take another drink, if only so I could break the intensity of his stare. It felt like he could see into the very heart of me.

"Your curse. You've been so focused on helping everyone else that you seem to have forgotten it exists. You're not mad at Jostein for taking it from you. You don't seem at all bothered that putting it back in the mines means you'll never get to leave this place."

"Oh. Well, I didn't really think it was a question. I'd never choose my freedom over the future of Steingard and all the rest. Besides, you told me you'd find another way."

"You are a beautiful person, Astrid Balstad. And I've been a fool not to sweep you off your feet."

Tormund tugged me close and kissed me. My toes curled as his lips swept across mine, the delicious scent of his shadows pressing into me. Then he quite literally swept me off my feet. His hand slipped down the length of me and cupped my backside. Lifting me off the ground, he carried me to the wall and pressed me up against it, his tongue still exploring my mouth.

I moaned and slid my fingers into his hair, relishing the silken strands.

He stiffened against me. "Gods. What I would give to feel you touch my horns."

Heat stormed through me, pulsing between my thighs. Answering his invitation, I dragged my hand across the top of his hair, then gently touched his left horn. It was smooth and almost silken, just like his shadows. Tormund shuddered, groaning in pleasure.

With a smile, I caressed the length of it. Tormund grabbed my right hand—the one not touching his horn—and trapped it against the wall. His shadows darted out, pulling at my tunic, at my trousers. Before I understood what was happening, they'd ripped my clothes right off my body and then did the same to his.

I gasped, the cool air sweeping across my peaked nipples.

His gaze dropped to my breasts. Hunger lit his eyes. "You are the most beautiful creature I've ever seen."

My heart pounded. I was all too aware of his bare skin against mine, the wetness coating my thighs, and his hard length pressing against my stomach. Tormund leaned in and nicked my skin with his teeth.

Still shuddering, he murmured into my ear. "I want to take my time with you. I want to caress every inch of your skin and memorize every curve.

But you touching my horns has driven me to the brink of insanity. I need you now, Astrid." He pulled back and met my eyes. "May I take you?"

I swallowed and nodded. Without needing any further encouragement, Tormund groaned and slid inside me. My walls tightened around him, answering his need with my own. He pulled back and thrust hard, trembling as he moved, like he was barely holding on to his control.

"I want you," I murmured against his cheek, dragging my hand up the length of his horn.

"Fucking fates." He thrust into me harder, faster, gripping my thighs and my wrist. My backside hit the wall, the cool stone a contrast to the heat of Tormund's skin. I dragged my hand down his horn again.

He growled and thrust harder, building the pleasure in my core. When he loosened the grip on my wrist to hold my hip, I reached up and clung to his other horn. Now that I held on to both of them, he broke.

He pushed into me, harder and faster, growling with ferocious abandon. His cries of pleasure tore out of the tavern, echoing across the Endless Chasm, but I didn't care. Everything in me coiled tight, an explosion of delicious pleasure threatening to shake through me.

I was so close to release. I was almost there.

Tormund pounded into me. His length hit just the right spot and—my core throbbed. Powerful quakes tore through me. Tormund groaned when he felt my pleasure, and he thrust again—twice, then a third time—and his own release followed mine.

For a moment, neither of us spoke. We merely held on to each other, sweat glistening on our bare skin. Eventually, Tormund lowered me to the floor, but he snatched away my clothes when I went for them.

A wicked glint lit his eyes. "You can put these back on if you promise me I can take them off again when we get to your cottage."

"You want to stay with me in my cottage?" I asked, still breathless from the act.

"I would like nothing more." He slid his finger beneath my chin. "But only if you want the same."

Warmth bloomed inside me. "There are quite a lot of plants in my cottage. They might not want to share."

"I'm certain we can manage." He winked. "Besides, there are things I'd like to do, and I'd rather we not have an audience."

Already, my core tightened. Need burned through me, so overwhelming I was tempted to stroke his horns again, just to get him going. Now that I knew what he liked, I wanted to do it a million times.

"I quite like the sound of that," I said.

He slid his hand along my curving hips. "Only problem is, you are perfection, love. I'm not sure I can wait."

"I think I hear some drunk dwarves coming," I told him, pointing out the door when another round of singing reached my ears. They couldn't be more than a ledge or two away, which meant they might be coming here.

"Hmm, that would definitely get in the way of what I want to do."

Tormund held out a hand, and I took it. And then I led him back to my cottage, where I showed him my plants, my bed, and anything else he wanted to see. It turned out he wanted to see it all.

23

ASTRID

I'd never had a better night's sleep in my life. Tormund's chest rose and fell beneath me, the steady rhythm of his heartbeat like a song that called to my soul. I nestled into his shoulder and loosed a contented sigh. Regardless of the loss I had to face, I thought I could be happy here like this. My dream of grass and sunlight would always stay with me, but I could learn to be content without it.

I could be content with *him*. If only he could stay.

His breathing changed, and a moment later, he brushed a kiss across my forehead. Something about it felt far more intimate than anything we'd done the night before.

"Good morning," he murmured against my hair.

"Morning to you, too."

"You feel awfully nice pressed against me like that," he said, his voice rough with meaning. "If I had my way, we'd stay in your bed all morning, all day, and all night again."

I giggled. "Might get a tad hungry if we never left the bed."

"Then I'd just find some food and deliver it to you. You could even lick it off my chest if you'd like."

"Only if you promise to lick it off mine, too," I said bravely.

I'd never spoken to anyone like this, but something about being in his presence gave me a burst of confidence. In fact, I felt like I could say or do anything, and he'd not only refrain from laughing, but he'd welcome it eagerly.

Gods, it felt good to be wanted. I'd never really felt special before. Sure, I was one of the unlucky few who lived with a curse, but it didn't make me different from anyone else when it came to what mattered. I was just a normal woman with a normal job who liked normal things. And I was fine with that. I never really wanted to be anything else.

But to be special in the eyes of someone else… well, it felt bloomin' good, all right?

I rolled onto my stomach and gazed up at him, swatting aside a vine crawling toward the bed. "I worry if we get up now, this will all turn into a dream."

"I can promise you this is very real." He tucked a curly strand of hair behind my ear. "Just like everything you make me feel. No matter what happens, I want you to remember that."

My heart pounded. "Are you going to leave The Deep?"

"Not just yet."

"But eventually, you'll have to go." I searched his eyes for confirmation. "You have to search the world, far and wide, for Tahir."

"For you, too, Astrid," he murmured, trailing his fingers up and down my bare arm. "There has to be a way to help you both. And I *will* find it."

I looked away. "I'd rather…" I blew out a breath, suddenly unable to say it for fear he'd turn me down.

I'd rather you come back here after you help Tahir. Don't worry about my freedom. Just come home to me.

"What is it, Astrid?" he asked. "You know you can tell me anything."

I dragged my gaze back to his face. The earnestness in his expression took my breath away. "It's a silly thing to say and wrong of me to ask it of you."

He cupped my cheek. "Just say it."

"I'd rather..." My voice broke off. I cleared my throat and tried again. "I'd rather you came back to me than spend years away from here, searching for a cure. But like I said, it isn't fair for me to ask that of you. You'd be as stuck in the mountains as I am."

"I'd gladly give up the sun if it meant I could have you," he said without a moment of hesitation.

I shuddered out a breath. His thumb caressed my jaw, heat trailing in its wake. I shook my head, his words beyond my comprehension. "How can you say that?"

"Because the sun has never made me feel the way that you do, Astrid Balstad," he murmured. "Now come here. I want to hold you before we have to go bribe a dragon to give us all her gold coins."

I laughed, lowered my head to his chest, and breathed in the scent of him. His fingers trailed up and down my arms, his shadows curling around my legs. Every single inch of me he touched, holding me with more care and attention than I'd ever dreamt he could give. I had been so wrong about him, from the moment we'd met. He gave off the impression of someone who thought he was better than everyone else. Someone who would ground others into dust.

But all that attitude and swagger hid the truth—he was as soft and gooey inside as melted chocolate.

I smiled against his skin. He was as delicious as chocolate, too.

"What are you grinning at down there?" he asked, his voice rumbling against me.

"Just thinking about chocolate," I said, smile widening even further.

"Wow. I feel like I should be insulted, but I wouldn't mind some chocolate, too. Please tell me you have some stashed somewhere in this house."

"If I did, the plants would have already gotten to it," I replied.

"Excellent point." His stomach emitted an impressively loud growl. "See? Chocolate is sorely needed."

I sat up and instantly regretted the space I'd made between us. "I suppose that's our cue to find food and pack our bags. The sooner, the better. I don't want to leave everyone in the dark for longer than necessary."

To punctuate my statement, my stomach rumbled with displeasure. I hadn't eaten since yesterday. Or whatever day it was. I no longer knew.

"As much as I'd prefer you to climb back on top of me, I can't very well let you starve, now can I?" With a groan, he pushed up from the bed. When he met my eyes, a spark went through my core. "We have some unfinished business, and don't you forget it."

"Does this unfinished business involve me climbing on top of you?"

"Yes, exactly. Ideally, over and over again. So many times that you forget your own name."

My entire body flushed. "I like the sound of that."

24

ASTRID

"Morning, Yulla. How much beet sugar do you have?" I stood on the front stoop of my friend's cottage. All the windows were dark. She rubbed at her red-rimmed eyes, seemingly oblivious to the fact she was leaning against her doorframe in nothing but a slip. Behind her, toddlers screamed and chased each other through the house.

"I have no idea, Astrid. Why are you asking me about beet sugar?" she asked tiredly.

"I need to make a very large batch of moss cakes," I told her.

She squinted at me. "How? All the sunstones are dead."

"I'll explain later." I leaned sideways and

peered into her house. "So, about that sugar. You got any? I'll find a way to pay you back."

"Sure, sure." She motioned me inside. "But don't you worry about replacing it. Not like we'll ever get to use it again, right? Without the sunstones, we'll never bake again."

"Hmm. We'll see about that." I ignored the question in her eyes and darted through the rush of charging children. The kitchen was a mess. Pots and pans were scattered on the floor, and bread-crumbs dotted the dining table. Empty tankards were piled beside a carton of eggs that looked like they'd been smashed against the wall. Yolk oozed down the stone.

"Um, Yulla," I asked carefully. "What happened here?"

"Oh, that." She waved at the mess. "The children were panicking about the dark, so I tried to make them laugh. It turned out smashing eggs on the wall did the trick." Sighing, she plopped onto one of the kitchen chairs. "Honestly, I will do anything at this point for a moment of calm with them. I will dance on my head wearing fish on my feet if I must."

"That's…quite the mental image."

"A funny one, right?" She loosed a tired laugh. "It'd probably work to entertain them. You got any fish?"

I grinned. "Can't say I do, but I'm heading to Rockheim. I bet they've got some I can bring back for you."

Two lines creased the skin between her eyes. "Wait, you're leaving Steingard already? You didn't even ask me where I'm planning to move!" She swatted my arm, but I could see the hurt on every inch of her face. She'd thought I'd decided on my next home without asking her where she wanted to go. A fond warmth flooded through me. Bloomin' fates, I'd been so focused on freedom that I really had lost sight of everything I already had. Yulla was like family, and she felt the same about me.

"Ah, my love." I threw my arms around her shoulders and hugged her tight against me. "I'd never move somewhere unless I knew you'd be there, too."

She pulled back, sniffling. A few damp spots were splattered across her cheeks. "Then what in fate's name are you going to Rockheim for?"

"I'm going to fix our sunstones, all right?"

She frowned. "But how? No offense Astrid, but I don't see how you going to Rockheim solves a damn thing."

"It's a long, long, *loooong* story."

She squinted at me. "Wait a minute. You look all flushed. And don't you pretend that Tormund didn't spend the night in your cottage last night. I saw him go in there, looking all horny."

I nearly choked on my saliva.

"That didn't come out quite right. I meant his horns." She tapped her forehead, then grinned wickedly. "Though by the look on your face, I'm guessing I wasn't far off the mark."

"I…" My words were strangled in my throat. I had no idea how to answer that. Yulla and I told each other *everything*—and I do mean everything. Lying to her wasn't an option. But things with Tormund were so new and delicate that I didn't even know how to talk about it yet.

"My gods." Yulla clapped. "You *did* get cozy with him, didn't you? Tell me everything. What was he like? Did you play with his horns? Tell me you played with his horns."

"Yulla, I swear I'll tell you everything. *Later.* Right now, I need that beet sugar so I can save the sunstones."

A spark lit her eyes, and she sprang to her feet as if she'd been injected with the sugar. It was as if all she'd needed was a little bit of hope. And fates be damned, I'd actually been the one to give it to her.

After everything she'd given me over the years.

I blinked back my own tears and watched her bustle around her kitchen. She drew out five large bags of beet sugar and deposited them in my arms.

"There." She stepped back and dusted off her hands. Sugar sprayed onto my face. I stuck out my tongue to catch a few stray flecks. Sweetness coated my tongue.

"Thanks. Mind opening the door? These are actually quite heavy."

"Yeah, but you're strong enough, aren't you? You big show-off." Winking, she bustled over to the door and opened it for me. "Too bad we had to call off the trials. I'm starting to think you might have actually been able to give the leaders a run for their money."

I opened my mouth to make a scathing retort about myself, just like I always did. Who did she think she was talking about? Little old me? I was no good at anything. I was weak. I would lose every task in such a humiliating fashion that the bard would come up with a new, demented song about me.

But then I snapped my mouth shut. Did I really still believe all that about myself? Perhaps I wasn't the *best*, but I wasn't the worst, either. Not by a long shot. Perhaps I could have won a trial or two if I'd really put my mind to it and trained.

If I'd actually *believed* I could do it.

But I'd never even given myself a real chance.

I'd just dismissed any hope of succeeding, to the point where I'd decided I shouldn't even bother trying. What could I have accomplished if I hadn't done that? How well could I have done if only I'd given it my all?

I shook my head. Not that it mattered now. This year's Fittest Under the Mountain had gone up in veritable flames, thanks to all this Everstone nonsense. If we were still in the northern mountains next year, hopefully we'd pick things up again, like they'd never ended. But for now, the games were off.

So I'd never get the chance to prove myself.

"I thought you didn't even want me to compete," I said to Yulla. "In fact, I distinctly remember you looking very panicked about it."

"Yeah, well." She shrugged, patted me on the cheek, and then tossed me another bag of sugar. It landed on top of the others with an inexplicably heavy *thump*. "I underestimated you, which I should have never done. You're Astrid Balstad, for fate's sake. I've never met anyone who works in the mines as hard as you do. I should have backed you, my love. Should have bet the bloomin' lot of gold on you winning at least one trial." She cocked her head, considering me. "Maybe the one where they steer the mine carts around. Bet you'd be damn good at that."

"I'd probably do all right with that one." I grinned. It felt weird to say something positive about myself, like I was bragging. But I knew Yulla wouldn't see it that way.

"Damn straight. Now go on. You said you're trying to fix whatever's going on with our sunstones. I don't know how you plan on solving it with beet sugar, but I'm pinning all my hopes on you. You've got this, my love."

And with that, I took her hopes and her belief in me and walked out with enough sugar to make at least a hundred moss cakes.

"**W**hat else do we need?" Tormund asked, eyeing the mine cart full of baking supplies.

I'd managed to conjure up quite a lot of cave wheat flour, eggs, stalagmite milk, rum, and well over twenty baking trays. Every time I'd knocked on a door, a frantic and wide-eyed dwarf peered out, afraid I was there to give them even more bad news. And once I filled them in on my plan to fix things with moss cakes, life returned to their eyes, they rummaged around in their house, and donated as much as they could possibly find.

Now Tormund and I had over five mine carts packed with food and baking supplies. I could only hope my plan—which was admittedly ridiculous—would work. The idea of returning to Steingard and the other nearby villages and telling them I failed… well, it wasn't an option. I couldn't stand the thought of seeing that resigned sadness filling every face again.

No one wanted to leave their homes and move somewhere else. Their lives were here. Everything—and everyone—they knew and loved were in these cottages dotted around the chasm. To upend everything, to find somewhere new, to start all over again…

Some people loved to wander. And some found a corner of the world they loved, curled up in the warmth and familiarity of it, and found a happiness so bone-deep they yearned to stay forever.

I was beginning to realize most of the people I knew were the latter. And I might be the latter, too.

Gods, I bloomin' loved this place. I loved The Wet Beard with its booming laughter and ridiculous songs that I could hear while I worked. I loved the sticky tabletops and the sunstone glow and the brew, even if it wasn't near as good as Lilia's.

I loved my cottage with its cool stone walls and cozy loft. And my plants, all two dozen of them, battling for dominance and eating all my damn food. I loved Yulla and how her voice echoed through the chasm when she called out to me every morning. I loved the feeling I got in my mind and my bones after a long day collecting sunstones for my village. The pride I felt when I replaced another, contributing something important to those I loved.

I even loved the bloomin' chasm and the breeze that flowed through it, carrying the scent of the daisies through every village that clustered around it.

It was home.

It was good.

And it was *mine*.

Tormund ducked his head before me. "You all right? You've gone quiet."

I smiled up at him. "I'm fine, Tormund. I just...I think I'm finally understanding what you've been trying to tell me all this time."

He brushed my hair away from my face. "And what's that?"

"I don't need freedom to be happy. I have everything I could ever want here in these mountains with the people I love and the home I'm lucky enough to have." I shook my head. "I truly don't know why I've been so determined to get out of here."

Tormund's smile went wide. He stood tall and

leaned back on his heels, sliding his hands into his trouser pockets. "It's about damn time."

"I know. It shouldn't have taken the death of the sunstones to make me realize, but…there really is nothing more important to me than this place and its survival. I can't imagine living anywhere else."

He cocked his head. "Say it, then."

"Say what?"

"Tell me about your curse. Say the words out loud."

"But I can't do that." I frowned. "If I could, I would have told you about my curse when you first asked me why I was so determined to find the Everstone."

"Ah ha!" He laughed out loud, his face lighting up. "You just said it. See?"

I stared at him blankly. "What are you talking about?"

"You just said the words. 'My curse.'"

His meaning hit me like a mine cart full of sunstones. Until now, I'd always had to tiptoe around the truth, even with people who knew about the curse. Even with Lilia, who had somehow extracted every nugget of information I had about it. All these years, I'd never been able to even mutter the word 'curse' to her. At least not when referencing myself.

And yet, I'd just said it out loud. Nothing had

stopped me. My tongue hadn't twisted; my mind hadn't gone blank.

"My curse," I repeated, revelling in the way it tumbled out of my mouth so easily. "My curse."

I pranced from one end of the mine to the other, tossing faded sunstones into the air. "My curse, my curse, my curse!"

Tormund laughed and chased after me. He caught me by the middle and tugged me into his chest, his shadows whorling around me in victorious laps. "You know what this means, don't you?"

"I can go outside," I said breathlessly.

"You can go outside," he said, beaming.

But then my happiness dimmed. "I meant what I said. I want to stay here. This place is home, and I don't need to see the world beyond any longer."

"I know." He dropped a kiss on my nose. "That's why it's worked. You've accepted your lot. You've embraced it. And now, Astrid Balstad, you get to see the sun."

25

ASTRID

"Later," I told him, begrudgingly extracting myself from his embrace. "Right now, there are moss cakes to bake."

He grunted and watched me with tormented eyes as I fussed with the mine carts, hooking them together with metal chains. By the time I was through, he still hadn't moved from his spot.

"You know, it's ironic," he said, his voice deep and dark. "I want nothing more than to take you above ground right now so we can pack a picnic and watch the sunset together. I want to show you exactly how amazing I think you are. But the reason I feel that way is because you *aren't* going to do that with me right now. You're not choosing yourself. You're choosing your people. And that's what makes me want you so badly."

I flushed, all the way from my cheeks to the growing ache in my core. Every time he complimented me, it felt like the first time. "Just hold on to that thought, because your plan sounds very nice to me."

"We can even take some of your moss cakes since you like them so much," he said with a grin.

"You can admit you like them. I won't tell anyone."

"They are luminescent," he said. "No one in their right mind would like one of those things."

"Good thing you're not in your right mind." I giggled. "You walked straight into that, you have to admit."

"Hmm. Proud of that one, are you?"

"Very."

"You're lucky you're cute."

Giggling again, I moved to the front mine cart and grabbed the yokes. "How cute, exactly?"

"So cute I could ravish you and never tire of it." As if to punctuate his statement, he leaned in, skimmed his teeth across my neck, and nipped my skin. A moan curled from the depths of my throat, and the temptation to drag him into the mine cart was so overwhelming I nearly gave in and did it.

"Later," I said, more to myself than to him. And as we began our trek down the mines, I envisioned exactly what later might feel like.

When we reached the hole in the tunnel floor, I realized how badly my plan had, erm, *holes* in it, so to speak. We'd had to drag the carts behind us after a while since the tracks didn't lead here. Sweat dampened my forehead, and my muscles ached from use, but we'd made it by taking turns. Dragging five connected carts across an uneven stone ground was no easy feat, but it wasn't an impossible one.

But getting them from here to the bottom of the cavern below most definitely was.

"We need to use the ropes and make a pulley system." I tugged a curved metal piece from my pack and showed it to Tormund. "It'll take a while, but it will get everything down there safely."

Tormund grinned at me. "Smart woman."

"I'd like to say it was my idea, but it wasn't. We use pulley systems like this all the time in the mines to—"

"Astrid," Tormund said. "You're doing it again. You don't need to downplay your smarts or your talents around me."

My chest lifted, and then I nodded. "Right. Thank you, then."

Together, we wound the rope through the metal

and constructed the pulley. It took well over an hour, perhaps even more, to lower all the mine carts to the bottom cave. By the time we were done, sweat coated every inch of me, seeping into the sleeves of my tunic. My hair had transformed into damp ringlets—without the bells. I'd learned my lesson from last time. Tormund looked like he'd barely broken a sweat. Even though he was a shadow demon, his ability to do pretty much anything just as easily as if he were lounging around eating cake was impressive, to say the least.

"All right, come on. Let's go." I shoved the mine cart across the rocky cave floor.

Tormund followed, grabbing the sides to help me steer it across the uneven surface. We reached the crack in the wall that led to the dragon's lair only a few minutes later. Sighing, I leaned against the cart and wiped a new layer of sweat from my brow.

"This is hard work," I muttered. "Why do you still look like you could run the entire length of this cavern and back a hundred times?"

He frowned and shifted on his feet uneasily. "Shadow demons have a lot of stamina." Then he winked.

I laughed in response, which seemed to erase whatever unease he'd felt a moment before. He knelt and peered through the crack we needed to traverse to reach the dragon. But I frowned as I watched him. He hadn't liked my question, which hadn't even been a question. More of a joke, really. And yet something about it had put him on edge, like he didn't want me to know the truth of his powers.

Was he keeping something from me?

I didn't want to think it. After everything we'd shared, it felt like all the walls between us had come crashing down. He knew *everything* about me. And despite not speaking it out loud yet, I'd given him my heart.

Had I been wrong in thinking he'd given me his?

Tormund backed out of the crack and brushed the dirt off his sleeves. "The dragon's not in there."

I blinked. That was the last thing I'd expected him to say. "Come again?"

"She's not there, but all her gold still is."

"But we..." I gestured at all the sugar, all the baking tins, all the moss. Hours upon hours had gone into preparation for this. We were here to gift the bloomin' dragon with hundreds of cakes, and she wasn't even here to eat them! I am a pretty level-headed person most of the time, but right then, I could have screamed.

"I'm certain she'll be back. A dragon would never leave a pile of gold for longer than a few hours. She's probably out hunting." Tormund scratched the base of his horns, then pointed at the pond in the far corner of the cavern. "We can have a drink and rest until she gets back."

"I don't want to rest," I said. Not that it mattered what I wanted. If the dragon wasn't here, there wasn't much we could do. We could *steal* the gold, of course, but I had no desire to anger a creature who could melt my skin from my bones. I would rather wait and supply the moss cakes, thank you very much.

I trailed after Tormund, still watching him carefully. He sauntered along no differently than normal. Perhaps I'd read his earlier reaction wrong. It was dark down here, and I was tired, and there really was no reason for him to feel uncomfortable with a comment about his power.

When we reached the pond, I settled onto a flat rock beside it and dipped my fingers into the cool water. I splashed my face, then drank a palm-full, sighing as the water slid down my parched throat. As much as I hated to admit it, I needed this rest.

"We have a long road ahead of us after this," Tormund said. "Feel free to take the opportunity to bathe. If you'd like."

I lifted my gaze to meet his. He was staring at me with a dark, hooded look. Shadows whorled around him. "Are you saying I smell?"

"I'm saying I wouldn't mind watching you strip naked and bathe while we're waiting. We don't know how long before we reach another pond like this."

Biting back a smile, I tugged my tunic over my head and dropped it by my feet. We'd likely pass another pond or lake within hours, but the look of utter desire on his face made me want to keep that little fact to myself. Boldly, I unbuttoned my trousers and pushed them down.

Tormund watched my every move with eager eyes.

My belly jiggled as I stepped over the side of the pond and slipped one foot into the water. Its cool embrace soothed my sweat-soaked skin, goosebumps pebbling my arms. A shiver went through me, and my nipples tightened.

Tormund sucked in a breath and stood. "Gods, you're beautiful."

With my eyes locked on his, I slid my other foot into the pond, lowered myself to my chin, and then stood back up. Rivulets of water trailed down my skin, streaming across my breasts. A hiss went through Tormund's lips.

"Is there a problem?" I asked him sweetly.

"Come here," he said in a rough voice, pointing at the flat stone.

Heat tightened my core, though the rest of me

was cold, my bare skin covered in goosebumps. "If I get out of the pond, I'll have to get dressed. It's not very warm in this cave."

"I'll keep you warm," he said—*demanded*, really. But when he held out his hand, there was a question in his eyes. And I answered yes by sliding my fingers through his.

Tormund tugged me out of the pond and gently pressed on my shoulders to lower me onto the stone. I sat, sucking in a breath when he knelt between my thighs. With gentle fingers, he nudged my legs wider before him. My core pulsed with a delicious ache.

"Is there something that you'd like?" Tormund asked as he stared up at me through my parted thighs.

I swallowed, my heartbeat thrumming in my neck. "I think so, but I've never done this before. What you're about to do, I mean. I've done other things. Well, you know that, because we did it."

I realized I was rambling nervously, so I shut my mouth.

"Hmm." He murmured it against my skin, the sound sending shockwaves of need through my body. "We must remedy that immediately. Relax against the stone, Astrid. Let me show you what it means to be wanted by a shadow demon."

He brushed his lips against my thigh. I gasped

and dug my fingernails into his shoulders. Smiling, he dragged his tongue across my skin and then stilled just beside my core. And then he licked me. An explosion of pleasure shook through my body. Tormund groaned, as if he liked my reaction, as if my thrill gave him a bolt of pleasure, too.

He licked me again, sliding his tongue across the core of me. Gods, this felt good. I dropped back my head and moaned as he drove his tongue inside me, slipping back and forth across my bud. I shuddered. An intoxicating pleasure built inside me, tightening and tightening and *tightening*.

And then he flicked his tongue across my bud, and I shattered completely.

I gasped, pulses shaking through me. Chest heaving, I started to move away from him, but Tormund grabbed my legs and held me in place against his mouth. His tongue darted out again, and another round of quakes went through me.

When they finally subsided, I collapsed onto the stone, feeling more content and more relaxed than I'd ever felt in my life.

And then Tormund lowered his body on top of mine, desire flickering in the depths of his midnight eyes. My core tightened again in anticipation, sooner than I would have thought possible. He dropped his mouth to mine and kissed me with a ravenous hunger that made my toes curl.

"I hope you don't mind that I'm not finished with you just yet," he purred.

I took his hand in mine and put it between my thighs. "Do I feel like I mind?"

"You feel soaking wet, love." His teeth skimmed my neck, and a delicious heat sparked in their wake. "Tell me you want me."

I reached up and stroked his horn. "I want you."

I gasped when he took my leg, lifted it over his shoulder, and hooked it behind his neck. Then he slid inside me, his eyes locked on mine. Everything else dropped away. The only thing in this cave was him and me and the delicious heat building between us.

Tormund pushed into me. I arched against him, crying out when his length hit the very back of me. With an encouraging grunt, he grabbed my other leg and put it on his shoulder. Thrusting inside me once again, he consumed every part of me.

Then his pace slowed. He worked himself inside me in low, sensual strokes, his body moving against the delicate bud he'd only just licked. It was almost too much to bear. My moans filled the cavernous space, echoing all around us. Every time he thrust, I bucked against the rock. All control of my body was gone. I was putty in his hands.

Suddenly, Tormund pulled back and flipped me

around. He stood behind me and lifted my arse in the air. Angling his length, he grasped my thighs and slammed into my pussy from behind.

"Oh my gods," I managed to eke out, stars dotting my eyes. This felt even better than the other position, and that had felt pretty bloomin' good.

Tormund dug his fingers into my hips, his thumb caressing my arse. He tugged me into him just as he pounded inside me once more. Overwhelming pleasure crashed through me.

He slid himself out and pushed his finger inside me, wetting his finger. Reaching around to my front, he slid his finger across my aching bud and thrust inside me. The combined pleasure lit up in the backs of my eyes.

"That's right," he murmured. "Come close to the edge, love."

He drove into me again and stroked me. I shuddered, my hands curling against the stone. Holding me in place, he quickened, his thrusts faster and harder now. I lifted my arse higher, desperate for release.

"You take me so good, Astrid. Everything you do is perfect."

At the sound of my name on his tongue, I careened over the edge. Pleasure tore through my core, throbbing so hard I thought I might shatter into pieces. I panted and gripped the stone, my heart racing, my body shaking as hard as my quakes.

Tormund held still while I finished, groaning every time my walls tightened around his cock. When my orgasm was over, he gripped my hips again, gently moving in and out. "I don't want to push you too hard. Is this all right?"

In answer, I lifted my arse even higher. With an appreciative growl, he thrust into me. A new wave of sparks filled my eyes.

"You can go faster," I breathed. "I want you to come, Tormund."

"I will do anything you want me to do." He thrust again. "I will take you, again and again, until you are fully satisfied." He thrust harder. "I will explore your pussy with my tongue. I will lick up every last drop." He slammed into me, all the way to the hilt. "And I will relish every inch of your beautiful body. I've served no gods before, but I will gladly serve you."

I gasped. No one had ever spoken to me this way. And while I knew some of this must be his lust talking, I didn't care. I leaned forward and pulled away from him, then lay on my back and pulled him to me. I wanted to see his face.

His heated eyes locked on mine. Spreading my legs, he pushed back inside me. He moved slowly at first, staring into the very heart of me. My heart thundered with every sensual thrust, and I moved my hips in time with his, like we were in a dance of our own making.

When he began to shudder, I reached up and dragged my hands up his horns, lingering at the tips. Tormund's pace quickened. A raw animalistic need tore through his eyes, and the growl he emitted resounded through the cave.

As the wild look in his eyes grew even wilder, so did my need to give him as much pleasure as he'd given me. I arched my back, grinding against his hips. I dragged my hands up and down his horns—faster, harder—until he gripped my hips and exploded inside of me.

Tormund roared. The ground shook. Rocks tumbled down from the walls, crashing into the pond and spraying water into my face. His shadows pulsed against my skin, faster and faster until—everything exploded.

Darkness took my mind.

26

TORMUND

Everything hurt. Groaning, I lifted my head from the ground and peered around with blurry eyes. Rocks were scattered around me, consuming what had once been the pond where Astrid had so gloriously bathed herself.

Shock jolted me. I leapt to my feet and nearly fell flat on my face, rubble crumbling beneath my feet. But the one thought blaring through my mind kept me standing.

Where the fuck is Astrid?!

Horror twisted my gut as I spun in a slow, agonizing circle. There was nothing surrounding me but boulders. What had once been a cavernous space was a tiny little cave now. I dropped to my knees. Rocks punched through my trousers, but I barely felt the pain.

Unshed tears burned my eyes. My power had done this. It had caused the entire cave to come crashing down on us, and…

I choked. My worst nightmare had come true. I knew I shouldn't have gotten close to her. I knew it would only ever end in this.

"Tormund!" a beautiful, sweet, perfect voice called out, muffled behind all this rock. I threw myself toward the sound.

"Astrid!" I pressed my face against the nearest boulder, my voice more panicked than I'd ever heard it. "Where are you? Are you hurt? Oh gods, I'm so sorry. I never should have lost control of myself like that."

"I'm still here beside the pond, Tormund. And I'm fine." A pause. "You're the one who's trapped."

Frowning, I eyed my surroundings again. What I'd thought was the pond was clearly nothing more than a pile of pebbles. In my panic, I'd seen things that weren't there. But none of that mattered. All I could imagine was Astrid shivering on the other side of these rocks, surrounded by boulders as big as a dragon.

"Are you sure you're fine?" I called out. "You can still move around all right?"

"It's like you drew all the falling rocks to your own body," she answered. "Tormund, what happened?"

I closed my eyes, lowered myself to the ground, and dropped my head against the boulder. "I…I've accidentally caused something like this before. People got hurt that time. I've never been able to forgive myself, because deep down I knew it would happen again." Heaviness settled onto my shoulders. "And I was right."

"All right. I see. But can you tell me *how* it happened? I've never heard of shadow demons having this kind of power. You brought down hundreds of rocks."

"I wish I could explain," I muttered.

"What was that?"

I cleared my throat and raised my voice. "I wish I could, Astrid."

A long silence answered. I could picture her face in my mind, putting the pieces of the puzzle together. How I'd known so much about curses. How cagey I'd been about my power. How I'd pulled away when we got too close and never had a good explanation for it. Astrid was a smart woman, and she knew how curses worked all too well.

"Well," she eventually said. "What kind of curse amplifies powers?"

"The kind that wants me to go through life never fully letting go," I said. "I have to remain tense. I have to keep a tight leash on myself and my emotions. Because this…this is what happens when I don't. I destroy everything I love."

Love. The word spilled from my lips. I swallowed, wondering if Astrid had noticed.

"Then you have to find a way to accept your powers for what they are," she said, sounding far too calm about this entire situation. "That's how you break your curse."

I laughed bitterly. "Astrid, this is it for me. I'm surrounded by boulders and piles of rocks. What just happened completely sapped my power. It will return to me eventually, but it could take days. I'm not strong enough to move all this stuff out of the way."

"That's fine," came the reply. "I'll move them."

I closed my eyes. Of course, she'd try to move all the rocks herself. It made me even more determined to protect her from me. "Astrid, you're better off without me in your life. Look what just happened. Next time, you could get hurt."

"I am not better off, thank you very much. You're just cursed, and we can bloomin' fix that," she snapped.

I frowned at the wall of stone separating us. "I don't want you to do this. The rocks could come crashing down on you if you try. Besides, you'd only be wasting your time. You need to get on with your quest for the sunstones. The dragon could be back inside her lair now."

"Ah, there it is." I could hear the smile in her voice. "You're trying to control everything. Well, you can't. I'm going to dig you out of there, whether you like it or not."

A scraping sound soon followed. I stood and paced the length of the cramped space, running my hands along the base of my horns. Astrid was better off without me. She didn't need my help to bake the moss cakes *or* deliver the treasure to Rockheim. In fact, she'd be safer without the threat of my powers crashing down on her—quite literally.

After a while, she called out, her voice a little closer now. "Have you thought about what I said?"

"I've been thinking that you're making a mistake."

She thumped the rocks. "No, we're not doing that. If I were you, what would you tell me?"

"Except I am not you, which is why I don't deserve you."

"You are a very infuriating demon."

"See? I don't deserve you."

"I can't wait to dig you out of these rocks, sit on top of you, and show you just how wrong you are."

My pulse pounded in my neck. Even in the midst of all of this, the thought of Astrid atop me, riding me, moaning at me, arching her back so her glorious breasts were in my face…it was almost enough for me to hope.

As if she'd picked up on that, she carried on. "I want to run my fingers along your horns and feel your tongue inside me."

"Fucking fates, Astrid," I muttered, going hard.

"But what's more, I want to wake up beside you every morning, nuzzle into your shoulder, and listen to your plans for the day. And then I want to come home to you after a long day in the mines. We can enjoy a nice home-cooked meal, trade stories, or just sit in comfortable silence from knowing each other so well. I want a future with you, Tormund, and I don't care if your powers are volatile. Because even when you lost control, you made sure I didn't get hurt. I think the truth is that your powers aren't as destructive as you believe they are."

My chest tightened. It felt like my heart wanted to leap out of me, shove the boulders out of the way, and run to her. Gods, what I would give to have everything she'd said. It was a nice, peaceful kind of life she dreamt of, one I could truly love. One where I could unravel all the twisted pieces of myself and finally be free.

But how could I do that if my power would destroy everything?

"What happened if I did this in your cottage,

Astrid? It would destroy your home and all your beloved plants," I said.

"Well, your power wouldn't do that if it's not powerful enough to do that, eh?" I could practically hear her rolling her eyes at me. "Listen to what I'm saying to you, you frustrating demon. Your power...it's only this strong because you believe it is. So stop bloomin' believing it!"

27

ASTRID

T his demon. I swore to the fates above that if he didn't listen to me, I was going to throw some moss cakes at him to knock some sense into him. It was like he couldn't see the truth of his own lessons. Ever since the day we'd met, he'd been telling me to *believe*. Believe in my own strength, believe in my own smarts, believe in my own skills.

Not only that, but he knew how curses worked. It was all about *acceptance*, too. He needed to accept what he'd done, stop believing he was going to destroy everything, and get his bloody arse out of that cave so he could sweep me off my feet and spend the rest of his life with me.

I let my annoyance fuel me. There was an

incredible amount of rocks between me and him, and some were quite large. I had to admit, I had my task cut out for me. There was a distinct possibility I could hurt myself trying, though I wouldn't tell him that until he was out of there.

The situation was this: there were two boulders —both about the size of me—squeezing together and forming a triangle with a boulder so large I'd dismissed it from my consideration. It wasn't going to move, no matter how much I believed in myself. After throwing on my clothes, I'd moved quite a lot of smaller rocks out of the way, but dozens more were piled on top of the big boulders. If I didn't move them first, they'd collide with my head. And I didn't think that'd be particularly enjoyable.

But instead of crying about it, I just got to work. First, I had to hoist myself up to the top of the boulder, where all the smaller rocks were. The rough surface scratched my palms, and my knees throbbed with pain from knocking against the stone. With only a couple of footholds, it was more of a scrabble than what I'd call a climb, but I eventually made it up there.

At the top, I grabbed a handful of rocks and started lobbing them across the cavern. It made quite a lot of noise, the *plunks* and *plops* echoing like the chorus of a hundred pickaxes. If the dragon was back in her lair and hadn't known someone was out there, she did now.

Hours passed like this. I had to take a lot of breaks. While I was a lot bloomin' stronger than I'd ever let myself believe, I was still just me without any enhanced shadow demon powers to keep me going for hours on end. I took a rest after a while, staying on top of the boulder. I'd made a big enough dent in the rocks to form a seat. But one moment's rest turned into two. Soon, I was drifting to sleep.

I was awoken by the sound of scrabbling. The *click, click, clink* of needles pierced through my veil of exhaustion, and as I blinked open my eyes, a jolt of shock went through me at the heavy darkness. For a moment, I tried to make sense of my surroundings. I wasn't at home, where the steady glow of sunstones illuminated my bed even in the deepest part of the night. In fact, this wasn't a bed at all. A hard rock jammed into my back.

Sucking in a breath, I sat up straight, and it all came flooding back to me.

Tormund needed me to dig him out of his makeshift cave, and I'd fallen asleep!

Bloomin' fates. When we got through this, Tormund would never let me hear the end of it.

Speaking of hearing…that clicking sound grew louder. It sounded like thousands of miniature pickaxes knocking against the ground. I frowned and squinted into the darkness. It couldn't be the dragon. She'd light up the whole room with her internal fire glowing beneath her scales.

So, what in fate's name could it be?

"Hello?" I called out.

More scrabbling answered. This time, it sounded like needles against metal rather than stone.

"The mine carts," I said in a gasp.

Whatever was happening, it was happening to our beloved carts with all the food and supplies we needed to gain access to the dragon's treasure. Something—or someone—was in here trying to get to it.

"Oh no you don't," I said through gritted teeth. And then, before I could think it through, I slid down the side of the boulder. A cry curdled in my throat as I flailed in the air, arms and legs swinging like flags getting twisted in a harsh breeze. My hair smacked my face, and a loud rip rent the air where my trousers got caught on the rock.

I hit the ground. Feet first, surprisingly. Gods, I

was a mess. I reached behind me to feel the extent of the damage to my trousers—and my pride, if I had to meet the dwarves of Rockheim like this—but I didn't get a chance to contemplate the severity of the rip.

Because spiders scuttled out of the darkness, surrounding me.

"Hmm."

There were well over a dozen of them. It was impossible to tell their numbers in the darkness. They looked a lot like my old friend, Daisy, though I didn't spot him in their midst. We were far from his favorite haunts, so he'd likely never even met this crowd. They might not be quite as friendly as him.

Several of them inched closer, their pincers clicking.

I held up my hands. "Listen. I'm just here passing through. I'm sorry if we've made a mess of your den, but we'll clean it all up." Perhaps I shouldn't have been aimlessly lobbing rocks everywhere. "No need for any, erm, *consuming,* if you get my meaning."

One of them cocked his head, his bulbous eyes glowing with hunger.

"Astrid," Tormund called out through the rubble, "please tell me you're not out there speaking to a spider."

"I'm afraid I can't tell you that," was my response.

A tortuous pause followed. "Is it the friendly one you tried to feed me to?"

"That would imply there was only one of them out here," I said, laughing in hopes it would release the tension in my shoulders.

"Right." His voice went sharp. "Get out of here and save yourself."

I watched the spiders, their pincers going wild. They scrabbled around the mine carts and poked at the contents. It seemed they realized it was something interesting but didn't quite know what to do with it.

"I think they're just hungry," I yelled.

"Don't you dare feed them any moss cakes," Tormund said. "Those are for the dragon."

"You have a lot of opinions for someone who wanted me to leave him behind a moment ago."

"You're damn right I do. Take the carts, run to the dragon lair, and make your bloomin' cakes."

I promptly ignored him.

"Hello, spiders," I said, approaching the over-sized beasts. Surprisingly, they scrabbled away from me, like they were afraid I might hurt them. I couldn't help but smile. See? They were only hungry. "I'd like to offer you a deal. Do you understand what I'm saying?"

The answer was some tip-tapping of pincers on stone. I took that as a yes.

"Good. Now here's what I'll give you." Then I filled them in on my plan.

Time was of the essence. Tormund had been right about that, at least. We still had a long journey to Rockheim if we wanted to make the trade, then another journey back. The dwarves in the northern villages needed to know they'd get their sunstones back, or they'd move on to somewhere else. I could eventually get Tormund out of all that rubble, but I'd barely made a dent in several hours. It might take days.

Days we did not have.

And so I conducted the spiders to scrabble up the stone wall, grab some rocks, and haul them to wherever they deemed best. Despite Tormund's frustrated commentary, the spiders seemed happy enough to have a task to do. In fact, they seemed to come alive with it, emitting a strange sound that was almost like a happy chirp.

When all the smaller rocks had been carried off the boulders, the spiders crawled behind the line of carts and blinked at me. I furrowed my brow at them in question. One scurried forward, tapped the massive boulder, and then shoved. The boulder didn't move, but his leg twisted at an odd angle, and he chirped—this time much less happily.

"Ah, I see," I said, nodding. "You can move the smaller ones easily enough, but your legs aren't strong enough for a big one like this."

I considered the boulder. It was pretty intimidating.

"Tormund!" I called. "I'm going to try something."

"Your voice has gone all high-pitched," he said slowly. "Are you sure whatever you're thinking is a good idea?"

"Nope!" I said with a laugh. "I need you to stand aside."

"Stand aside? Stand aside *where*?"

"Out of the way of the smallest boulder."

A long pause followed. "All right. I'm out of the way."

"That was surprisingly agreeable of you. You aren't going to try to talk me out of my plan?"

"You're going to roll the boulder far enough forward for me to squeeze through the crack," came his reply. "It's a good idea."

"And you're not going to tell me I should leave you trapped in there? Because of your cursed powers?" I raised my eyebrow.

"I just want to see your face again, Astrid. Fuck all the rest of it."

I smiled. Gods, I wanted to see his face again, too. It had only been a few hours, but it felt like years had passed. I wanted to bury my face in his chest and relish the scent of shadows against my skin. I wanted to feel his arms wrap around me, protective and steady and sure. And I wanted to look into his eyes and see the truth of his feelings. Neither of us had voiced it, but it was real.

I'd never been more certain of anything.

"You know, in the storybooks, it's the damsel who always needs saving," I said as I palmed the stone. "Feels kind of good to know the damsels can do the saving sometimes."

I swore I could *feel* him smile as I shoved the boulder. It took all my muscles straining, my heartbeat pounding as hard as it could, and my forehead drowning in sweat. But I pushed it, inch by inch, until a gap opened up large enough for Tormund to escape.

As soon as he stepped out, he swept me into his arms. My feet left the ground as he spun me in circles, clasping me against him like he was scared to let go, or else he'd never again touch me. I closed my eyes and buried my face in his neck, breathing him in. The scent of sweat and sunstone-kissed skin. But gone was the scent of his shadows.

I pulled back. "Did you do it? Did you listen to what I said?"

"I think my curse is broken," he murmured, pulling my lips to his. "All because I couldn't stand the thought of losing a life spent with you."

28

ASTRID

"Before we go in there, I need to tell you about my curse," Tormund said, steering me toward the pond. I sat on the flat rock once again and pulled my knees to my chest, waiting for his story.

He sighed before he began, pain evident in his eyes. "Just like you, I had this curse all my life. And like you, I felt the repercussions of it fairly young." Wincing, he glanced away. "I didn't know how to control my powers for a long time, and I was just a kid. You know how kids are. Wild and unfettered. Emotions are big."

I nodded. Yulla's children were boisterous, to say the least. They were an explosion of happiness and noise, or sadness and noise. So much life they had. I could only imagine how hard they'd find controlling a power like the one Tormund had been cursed with.

"I was at my aunt's one day, and she tried giving me some peas with dinner. I didn't much like peas." His mouth set into a grim line. "You can imagine where I'm going with this. My youthful anger exploded out of me. Rocks fell. My aunt survived, but she was badly wounded. Ever since, I knew I had to hold myself back. That's how I ended up training the way I have. I learned to use my power, but never more than what I could control. And I spent all my time in the mines. I forced myself to hide away from everyone, digging for gold without tools and carts and all the rest of it..."

"Tormund." I pressed my hand against the top of his. "You know that wasn't your fault."

He lifted his pained eyes to meet mine. "I know that. At least, now I do. I blamed myself for a very long time, and I've been terrified of doing it again—that or something far, far worse. And I nearly did."

"Except you *did* control it," I argued. "That's the only way the rocks would have fallen the way they did. We were *right beside that pond*. After the rocks fell, I was still by the pond. You were all the way over there, surrounded by all the rubble. That's not how rocks fall, Tormund, and you know it."

He squeezed my hand. "I do know it. And I also know it was my love for you that cut through the curse's bullshit and made sure I protected you from harm."

I sucked in a breath, my heart surging forward. He'd said it so casually, like it was just another word and not something as big as love. Like he didn't mean it the way I thought he had. But as his steady eyes gazed into mine, he nodded, a confirmation that what he'd spoken was true.

He loved me—really loved me. It seemed impossible, this amazing, powerful, wicked demon had swept into my life at exactly the right time and had shown me just how powerful I was myself.

My breath rattled in my lungs. I threw myself at him, wound my arms around his neck, and kissed him with a ferocious need building between my thighs. He clutched me against him, his mouth hot against mine. I didn't know how much time passed before we came up for air.

Pincers clicked on stone.

"Oh." Tormund laughed and slid his gaze toward the arena of spiders crowding around us. "We appear to have an audience."

"Well, I did promise them some moss cakes."

"Yes, I heard," he said, shaking his head. "Mind explaining how we're going to do that?"

"There are going to be a lot of promises involved. And a lot of baking," I admitted.

"Good thing you like baking, eh?"

"Not as much as I like you," I said.

A grin curled his lips. "That might be the cheesiest thing I've ever heard you say."

"You liked it, though, didn't you?" I asked, elbowing him in the side.

"I liked it enough that I'm now imagining all the things I want to do to you to see which one you like most," he said, his voice dropping to a near-growl.

Heat pulsed between my thighs. And without Tormund's shadows curling around me, I knew that every ounce of desire I felt was real and had nothing to do with his allure. Smiling, I hopped off the stone.

"Spiders and dragons and moss cakes first," I told him. "Sex later. Deal?"

"I'd rather it be sex now *and* sex later, but I'll take what I can get." He winked and wrapped his arm around my waist. And together, we left his rocky prison behind so that we could bribe a dragon.

I t turned out spiders were excellent at squeezing through tight spaces. They helped us move all the supplies out of the carts and onto the base of the dragon's gold coin mountain. As expected, she'd returned from her adventures and curled peacefully at the summit of her treasure. There appeared to be more gold coins than before, as well as a healthy amount of sunstones and a few other gems that oozed magic. Some of the sunstones still glowed, though most had run out of light, like the others.

"Hello," I called out, striding up the shimmering mountain. "You look like a dragon in need of some cake."

The dragon rose her head from the treasure and huffed. Gold rained down, a waterfall of clinking coins. Her eyes narrowed on us, but she made no move to attack. I took that as a positive development.

"Listen, you clearly like pretty things. So do dwarves." I shook my head. Wrong start. "Truth is, we like pretty things, like the sunstones, because we need them to survive down here in The Deep. They have the power to give us light and heat. Only problem is, someone accidentally traded away the source of that power. We need it back. But to get it back, we need something to offer them."

The dragon huffed again, but her tail had begun to twitch against the gold. She clearly saw where we were going with this.

"You have quite a lot of treasure, most of which I'm guessing came from an emerald stone. Am I right?"

A moment passed without an answer, and then she nodded.

"Good. That's great."

"Is it great, though?" Tormund murmured in a low voice from beside me.

"Well, it means there's a lot of gold to go around. We were hoping we could take some of it —whoa!" I stumbled back as the dragon's head soared toward me. Hot air blasted into my face.

Tormund grabbed my arm and threw me behind him. He bent his knees and raised his fists, clearly planning to fight dragon fire with his bare hands. Fondness bloomed in my gut, despite the fear raging inside me.

"Stay back," he warned the dragon.

The dragon's head swooped closer but then careened to the side. She poked her snout against a mine cart and sniffed. A smile crept across my face.

"Ah, you've discovered our offering. In exchange for some of your treasure, we'll give you some moss cakes. We'll have to bake them here, of course, since all our heat is gone in Steingard. I figured we could use your flames?" Some scrabbling sounded behind me. "Oh, and I'm afraid we'll have to share some with these spiders here."

The dragon narrowed her eyes.

"If you like them, I will promise to bring you more," I said quickly. "A steady supply. For years to come. All I need is…five mine carts' worth of gold."

"And that gem, please?" Tormund pointed to a gem the color of diamonds, though there was something distinctly *not*-diamond about it. I cocked my head at him in question. He swallowed thickly. "That magic you feel coming off that stone? It's the same kind that caused Tahir's illness. I think it might be able to undo it, too."

My heart surged, and I turned back to the dragon. "Did you hear that? Tahir is a dragon, like you, and he would love to meet you and your siblings. But he can't, because he's trapped in another mountain. That gem right there? It might be able to set him free. And you get some moss cakes!"

I clasped my hands in front of me and fell silent, as much as I itched to ramble on, ticking off all the amazing facts about moss cakes. They were extremely high in various minerals that were important to a healthy body. Some of our dwarven scholars had done tests over the years. Those who regularly consumed moss cakes lived longer lives. Their wounds healed faster. They had more color in their cheeks, regardless of how much time they spent underground. Despite being a dessert, moss cakes were delightfully healthy.

But I doubted the dragon wanted to know any of this. So I merely said, "They're very delicious. Right, Tormund."

I stabbed my elbow into his side, and he coughed. I could have sworn his eyes watered as he muttered, "Delicious."

The dragon snorted into our faces, and the rush of her hot breath sent my hair streaming behind me. With the stench of her fire flooding my senses, I watched her shift back onto her haunches, nod once, and then poke the mine cart with her talon.

I could have cheered. In fact, I almost collapsed from the sheer relief of it all. My ridiculous plan had worked.

The dragon wanted some bloomin' moss cakes.

29

ASTRID

I returned to Steingard with five mine carts full of gold. As much as I'd wanted to carry straight on to Rockheim, I needed a fresh change of clothes and a pair of trousers that didn't have a massive rip in the arse. Dozens of dwarves were clustered around my front stoop, pacing and muttering with worry lining their faces. There was Yulla, of course, fussing over my plants. Jostein was there, too, sitting on my outdoor cot with his head in his hands. Several of the trial contestants were there, including Knut and Puldur. Tormund's friends, Meral and Altan, had come. Even Balder had shown up.

When the clattering of five heavy carts echoed through the chasm, every single head jerked our way. Jostein leapt to his feet.

"Ah, there you are!" Yulla called out cheerfully, and then she ran over and jabbed Balder's chest. "Told you she'd come back winning."

A silver-haired elf shoved through the plants that crawled across my front door and raced across the bridge. When she reached me, she flung her arms around me and pulled tight. Into my hair, she whispered, "I'm so glad to see you. Did you really find Hita?"

"Hita? Is that the dragon's name?"

"Yes." She sighed in relief. "She's one of Rivelin's. She went missing a few months ago, and he's been looking for her ever since. We were trying to find her when you left. I wish I'd known what you were up to, or we would have helped!"

"It's all right. We managed." And then I filled her in on everything that had happened.

When I finished the story, she hugged me tight, then said, "That's her, all right. She loves cake more than the rest of them. Thank you so much for finding her and for feeding her. Do you mind if I leave? I need to find my brother and tell him about Hita. He's worried sick."

"It's fine, Lil. I understand."

She searched my eyes, her brow furrowed. "You sure? I know the last few days have been a lot. Do you need any help travelling to Rockheim?"

A smile twitched the corners of my lips. "I have company."

She nodded, a spark of evil glee chasing away any sign of worry. "Yes, about that. I've heard some very interesting tidbits from Yulla about you two. And by the looks on your faces, all of it was true!"

She bounced up and down, clapping. A flush poured across my entire face. I was *extremely* aware that far too many of my friends were standing on the ledge, listening to this entire conversation. And if they hadn't been near enough to hear her voice, the chasm's echo would have done the job.

Word would spread fast if it hadn't already. Every dwarf in the surrounding villages would know Astrid Balstad had finally found a partner. But it was bound to get out eventually, especially when Tormund moved in and started a life with me.

I beamed up at him. He beamed right back. "All of it's true."

"I knew it." She clapped again, practically dancing down the length of the bridge. "The second you met him, I knew there was something about him you liked. Otherwise, he wouldn't have been able to get under your skin the way he did." She laughed. "Trust me. I know all about that."

"I'm sure you do." I patted her arm. "Now go on. Find Rivelin. I'm sure he's missing his dragon."

She thanked me again and scurried off. Tormund and I approached the others. They all clapped us on the backs, thanking us for finding enough treasure to bargain with the other dwarves. Meral and Altan teased Tormund about me, then exclaimed with happiness when he showed them the gem that could help Tahir.

Others drifted over as we told everyone our story until it seemed like the entire village of Steingard had come to hear the tale. Kegs were brought out. Ale was passed around. And, funnily enough, moss cakes started making the rounds.

It was only Jostein who avoided the festivities. He remained on my stoop, watching the celebration with despondent eyes. While Tormund welcomed some new arrivals and filled them in on our adventures through the mines, I ambled over to Jostein.

I settled onto the stoop next to him. He wouldn't even meet my eyes. "What's going on, Jostein? With the way you're acting, one might think you don't want us to trade the coins for the Everstone."

"No, no, I most definitely want that," he said quickly, then sighed. "I just hate it was my fault we lost it, and I made you go off to find a fix."

"I offered to do it," I said. "I was *happy* to do it, in fact."

"I know. You found a purpose. I always knew you would." He gave me a sad smile. "And I can also see there's something different about you now. There's a light in your eyes that wasn't there before. Some might think it's because of Tormund, but it's not, is it?"

"He's made me very happy, Jostein," I said quietly.

"But there is something else."

"Yes." I propped my elbow on my knee and put my tankard on the floor by my feet. Jostein had been acting so oddly since the start of the competition. And if I thought back, he'd been acting oddly before it, too. I'd wanted to pretend otherwise. He was the father I'd never known, but this sadness, this regret... "You never wanted me to break my curse."

He winced, his eyes trained on the daisies beside him. "No, I did not."

Frustration rattled through me like a vicious wind, even though I'd suspected it. "Why? You knew I wanted it more than anything."

"Because I am the one who asked the witch to gift you the curse," he said tightly, his hands gripping the sides of the stoop.

I hissed and pulled back. Surely I'd heard him wrong. *Surely* the man who'd raised me as his own wouldn't have trapped me here without any hope of ever moving on. Surely, surely, surely. Jostein loved me like a daughter. Didn't he?

"I'm so sorry, Astrid." He dropped his head into his hands. "After your parents died, the witch appeared. She showed me a future where you wandered the world for decades, so lonely you cried yourself to sleep every night. I couldn't bear it. And so I asked her to find a way to make you stay. Here, with all of us, your dwarven community."

"Jostein," I whispered, my heart pounding.

"I know it was a terrible thing to do, and it's caused you so much pain. I was just...I wanted you to be *happy*, and I thought you'd be happiest here, surrounded by all your friends and your plants. That's why I fed them all that moss cake the other day. I thought if you saw how much they thrived here, you'd want to be happy in Steingard." He lifted his head to meet my eyes, and tears tracked down his cheeks. "I was wrong."

The plants. Of course. I pressed my lips together. He had done a terrible thing, and a part of me wanted to hate him for it. But as I stared at his shaking shoulders and his genuine tears, I found I couldn't. He'd only done what he did out of love.

"And the Everstone? The competition?" I asked him.

He sniffled. "I entered you. I thought if you

competed for the 'stone' and lost, you might be able to give up your single-minded obsession with it. You were so focused on it that it seemed like you were missing out on life. All these years were passing by, and all you cared about was finding a way to break free of this place."

"Oh, Jostein," I sighed.

"I know you can never forgive me, and I know you'll leave as soon as the Everstone is back in its rightful place, but—"

"I'm not leaving, Jostein," I said quietly.

He looked up at me, raw hope in his eyes. "But you broke your curse. You're not bound to the mountains any longer."

"This is my home. I'm not leaving," I said, louder this time and firm enough that he knew just how serious I was. "I mean, I'll venture above to watch a sunset here and there, but I'm staying in Steingard."

"You're not leaving," he repeated.

"I'm not leaving," I confirmed, then held up a finger. "But I'm going to need you to promise you'll never make a decision about my life without my input again. No more entering me into competitions or asking witches to curse me. Next time there is any kind of problem, just...I don't know, *talk* to me about it?"

Tears gushed down his face. He laughed,

pulling me in for a hug. "You are far too understanding, my love, but I will gladly accept your forgiveness."

My stomach decided to respond by emitting a very obnoxious growl.

"Well, I will ask for one thing in return." I pulled back and eyed his leather satchel. "You got any chocolate?"

His booming laugh warmed my soul, and that was when I knew everything would be all right. We'd get through this. It might take some time to forget what he'd done, but I could never hate him. Especially since he was pulling three bars of chocolate from his bag.

He handed me the lot of them. "Don't tell anyone I gave you these. Or that I have loads more where those came from."

"*Loads* more?" I asked hopefully.

"Loads," he confirmed. "How many do you want?"

I grinned. "All of them."

ASTRID

As luck would have it, Rockheim met us halfway. They'd been on the return journey to their city when word reached them of our troubles. And contrary to what we'd assumed, they were more than happy to accept anything we could offer as a trade. So they'd stopped, turned around, and headed back our way to sort things out.

"The contract is written in blood, so we have to take something for the trade," the blonde dwarven woman said, her eyebrow piercing wobbling as she shuffled around the mine carts. "But you needn't have gone to all this trouble. We would have taken some moss cakes."

"Well, if you don't want the gold..." Jostein

tugged on the cart, but the Rockheim leader snapped out her hand and grabbed it.

She winked. "Didn't say that. Just remember we're your friendly neighbors next time, eh? We don't want your villages to descend into eternal darkness any more than you do. I'd hate to see anything bad happen to you, Jostein."

Jostein actually blushed.

We made the swap, returned home, and embedded the Everstone in an indentation Jostein indicated. Turned out, it had been hidden inside a tunnel near the melted tracks Tormund and I had found. Jostein had blocked off the entrance over a decade ago, which is how I'd never found it myself. He'd known it was there the whole time. And when I'd started poking around, he'd taken a torch to the tracks.

I chose to let it go. His plotting had caused me a lot of grief, but it had all worked out in the end. As soon as the Everstone took its rightful place, the orange-golden glow returned to every sunstone scattered throughout the northern villages. Almost in an instant, everything was right again.

Thank the fates for moss cakes.

Tormund led me to the watchtower and told me to wait while he vanished through the door leading to the outside world. I bounced on my toes, an anxious thrumming in my chest. I'd meant every word I'd said when I'd accepted my future and my fate. I didn't need to walk outside. I was content to never gaze at the sky or wander through fields of grass.

That didn't mean I wasn't excited now.

The door cracked open again, and light splashed onto the watchtower's stone floor. Tormund motioned me forward, delight dancing in his midnight eyes.

"Ready?" I swallowed.

"Come on," he said gently. "You don't need to be nervous."

I wasn't *nervous*, per se, but I'd built up this moment for so long that I was scared I might walk through that door and find the world was a muted gray, like all the stones. No more color. No more life. It'd all be gone.

"It's a beautiful spring day," Tormund said, waving me forward. "You can even see Rivelin's dragons soaring through the clouds, including our friend, Hita. I can't wait for Tahir to join them soon."

That finally got my feet moving.

Tormund widened the door, revealing a world full of splendor. I stepped out into air warmer than I'd ever felt, even with the breeze rustling the bells in my hair. The sky above was an endless stretch of blue, only interrupted by a smattering of puffy white clouds and dragon wings. I dropped back my head and closed my eyes, sunlight caressing my skin.

Everything within me sighed.

Birds chirped in the distance. Wind swept across my sun-kissed cheeks. The scent of brine rushed in from the sea beyond, and there—I could hear the rush of waves. It was everything I'd dreamt of and more, and yet I did not regret my choice to stay inside the mountains.

I'd happily come out here now and again, though.

Eventually, I opened my eyes to find Tormund gazing at me with stark adoration. His lips quirked up. "Happy?"

"Very." I beamed.

He nodded toward the ground. I'd yet to look at anything other than the sky. I now saw the patch-work blanket topped with a picnic basket over-flowing with food. My smile transformed from a regular one to one so wide my cheeks hurt.

"We get to eat out here?" I asked, jumping in place.

Tormund laughed. "We can eat and drink and dance all night. Soon, the sun will set, and colors will scrape across the sky like a painting. And then…" He winked. "We can do some other things I think you'll like."

I flushed. In the past few weeks, we'd been intimate almost every night, but I'd yet to stop blushing every time he spoke to me like that. I hoped I never would.

We settled onto the blanket. Tormund passed me a pastry I'd never tried before—something rich and salty packed with mushrooms and cheese. It was mouth-wateringly good. When I asked him about it, he said a human named Mabel had made it. I'd have to track her down and get the recipe one day.

Then we had potatoes slathered with butter, crispy carrots, and smoked fish. By the time we made our way through all that, my belly was full and my heart content. On the horizon, the sun inched lower. Streaks of orange lit up the sky, the color of sunstones.

"Beautiful," I murmured.

"It'll get even better than that," he promised, digging around in the picnic basket. A moment later, he extracted a smaller basket of moss cakes.

I giggled and slapped my hand against my

mouth. "I can't believe you brought those. You *hate* moss cakes."

"I could never hate the thing that brought us together and saved Steingard," he said solemnly.

"Can I ask you something? And you have to be honest." After hearing how that sounded out loud, I added, "It's nothing bad."

He squinted at me, clearly dubious. "Go on then."

I pinched the sides of a moss cake and held it in the air. "Have you actually tried one of these things?"

He opened his mouth, snapped it shut, and then found something interesting in the picnic basket. "Why would you ask me that?"

"Ha! I knew it." I waved the moss cake in front of his face. "You have to try it now, Tormund."

He grimaced. "It's a very odd color."

"What in fate's name is wrong with it?"

"It's the color of, well, *moss*. Have you ever eaten moss? It's not very good. Very grassy."

"No, I've never eaten moss by itself. Or grass. *Have you?*"

"Well, yeah, of course. When I was a little demon growing up, my friends and I dared each other to eat moss. And grass. And dirt."

I snorted. "You ate dirt?"

"I ate all manner of things. As a *child*," he said

grimly, then pointed at the moss cake. "Which is why I will not partake in that."

"If you loved me, you'd try it," I said in a singsong.

"Astrid Balstad," he said, inching closer to tickle my stomach. "That is thoroughly unfair."

His fingers slid beneath my tunic, and he tickled me mercilessly. I laughed, flailing against the blanket while the sky transformed into a sea of scarlet, violet, and amber. Pink splashed across it all, like someone had flung colors in random patterns. It made for the most beautiful sight of my life.

I stilled beneath Tormund, gazing up at it in pure awe. With this loving demon beside me, a belly full of delicious food, and a good, happy life, I wondered if my curse had ever truly been a curse. Because right now, I felt truly blessed.

And even if this was the last time I saw outside, it was enough. It was more than enough.

"I'll try your cake," he murmured, gazing down at me, "if it'll keep you smiling like that all night."

I reached to my side, found the basket, and curled my fingers around a fluffy cake. Then I held it in front of his lips so he couldn't back out of his promise.

"If you don't like it, I'll..."

"Yes?" He arched a brow.

"Do whatever you want in the bedroom," I said with a grin.

"Hmm. You're not making a good case for the cake. I already dislike it. Very, very much. And I am determined to continue to do so if that means I can hear you scream my name in pleasure."

"Good point," I admitted. "How about you just try it and tell me what you think?"

He sank his teeth into the green cake. I held my breath, waiting for a reaction, but none came. Tormund chewed slowly, cocking his head as if considering the flavor. Impatiently, I tapped my fingers against the blanket, wondering what was taking him so long. The immediate hit of beet sugar should have been enough to get him reaching for another one.

Eventually, he stopped chewing. And yet he remained mum.

"Well?" I asked. "Do you like it?"

"Do I like what?" He grinned wickedly.

I swatted his arm. "Do you like the bloomin' moss cake?"

"It's one of the strangest things I've ever eaten," he said.

I sighed. "All right. Well, I suppose you had to have *one* flaw."

"It's strange because it looks absolutely disgusting, but it might just be the best cake I've ever had."

I sat up straight, my jingling bells going wild. "You liked it!"

He laughed. "I suppose I did."

Giggling, I laid back down on the blanket and watched the colorful sky transform into shades of gold. "This is one of the best days ever."

"You don't think it could get any better?" Tormund asked.

"Right now, I can't see how."

"Then I suppose you wouldn't want to share this chocolate bar..." He leaned down with a square of chocolate pinched between his teeth. And when he brushed it across my lips, I took it eagerly, just as the wings of dragons flared across a golden sky.

EPILOGUE
ASTRID

ONE YEAR LATER

I chalked my hands and leapt for the metal rails. The Endless Chasm yawned beneath me, threatening to swallow me whole. But I barely gave it a second glance as I swung one hand in front of the other, quickly crossing the obstacle to the next ledge.

The crowd went wild.

Jostein had rearranged the order of the trials this year, just to shake things up. And this was the last one for the entire competition. If I won it, I won the whole thing. If I didn't, Knut would take the crown. And he was only a few rungs behind me.

Sweat coated the back of my neck, and my muscles screamed for a break. I wiped my face with a square of fabric I'd tucked in my waistband and scanned the obstacle ahead. I'd crossed the chasm. The only thing I had to do now was jump to the next rung, pull myself up and over, and then climb the rope to the watchtower.

Only.

This next move—pulling myself up and over the next rung—required a great deal of strength and skill. I'd spent the entire year training for it. And while I'd managed the feat a few times, I often failed. One wrong move, and I'd fall. Luckily, I'd only tumble right back onto this platform, but I couldn't win Fittest Under the Mountain without reaching that watchtower. Knut was definitely capable of it. And if not him, Pulder would do it. He wasn't far behind me, either.

I blew out a breath and flicked my hands by my sides. At this point in the competition, everything hurt. I'd heaved a boulder across an arena. I'd clattered along in a runaway mine cart, steering it to safety with pure grit and strength. I'd crawled on my hands and knees through muck. I'd even raced through tunnels, feet pounding stone, hands pumping at my sides. I had wrung out every last drop of energy from my tired body.

Thankfully, I'd had a square of chocolate before this task.

Would it help me get up and over? We were about to find out.

Shaking my shoulders, I nodded once to myself. I could do this. I'd done it before. Exhaustion didn't matter now. The screaming crowd behind me didn't matter, though knowing Tormund was there shouting my name gave me a burst of energy. His powers had eventually come back after that day in the mines, but they were muted compared to before. Still, he was good enough to have competed if he'd wanted to, but he'd chosen to sit in the stands and cheer me on instead.

His support had gotten me through my endless training, especially when I'd had to do it after long days working the mines. He'd helped me bake plenty of moss cakes to fuel my efforts—enjoying a few of the tasty treats himself. He's massaged my shoulders; he'd rubbed my feet. And he'd carried me home when I was too tired to walk.

He'd been the one to teach me how to do this. More than anything, I wanted to make him proud.

I took a deep breath. Eyes on the rung, I raised my arms and leapt. The rung came toward me. I ground my teeth and gripped it hard. Then I swung, throwing up my hips and pulling with every ounce of strength I had left. When weight-lessness pillowed my body, I threw my head forward.

The rung crashed into my hips, and my elbows bent at odd angles. But I was there. I was over the rung. Breath shaky, I climbed on top of the rung, grasping the rope before I fell.

Heart hammering my ribs, I began to climb. I could hardly believe it. I'd made it up and over, and I was almost there. The watchtower was so close now I could skim it with my fingertips.

The cheers were thunderous.

With every single muscle in my body aching, with every inch of my hands burning, I threw myself up the last few inches of the rope, scrabbled through the hatch above, and tumbled onto the floor of the watchtower. My breath heaved out of me, frantic and ragged. Sweat covered every inch of my skin, and I could barely see straight.

But it was worth it. Every bit of it was worth it.

Because I'd just won that trial. And that meant I'd won the whole bloomin' thing.

I held the champion cup over my head, basking in the cheers of an entire arena. All my loved ones were there. Jostein, Yulla, Lilia, and Ragnar. Balder, too.

They'd even made space for the dragons. Hita

perched in a corner of the arena with her mate, Tahir. They were both roaring their hearts out. Tormund's dragon friend had arrived in The Deep not long after Meral and Altan had taken the diamond gem to Azraak. The magic of the gem had worked. And he and Hita had been inseparable ever since.

Until a year ago, I'd never dreamt I could be standing here as the Fittest Under the Mountain. I'd never thought I could do something so hard, let alone win it. But if I'd learned something during my year of training, it was this: I could do hard things. Failure was always possible, but so was success. And I'd never discover which it was if I didn't try.

And so I'd tried my little heart out.

The Wet Beard swelled with drink and dancing. But of course, The Wet Beard always did. Ragnar, Lilia, Tormund, and I lifted our tankards, cheering the end of another day in the mountains. This one was special, of course, but I'd celebrated my win enough. I just wanted to enjoy a good evening with good people and good drink.

"So," Lilia said after we all sipped our ale and

our two partners wandered over to the bard stage to request a song. "Are you going to go after Galinn's record and try to win five in a row?"

"Once was enough," I said with a smile. "I've enjoyed competing, but I've had to spend the entire year so focused on it that I haven't been able to do much else. I'm happy to have a break and enjoy life with Tormund."

"I thought you might say that," she said with a nod in Tormund's direction. "How are things going with him?"

"He makes me happy," I said.

"Good. Because I think he's coming over here to ask you something." With a laugh, Lilia jumped to her feet and vanished into the throng.

I twisted toward Tormund. He was heading my way with a serious look in his eye. Ragnar had hung back by the stage, where the bard had started plucking a very familiar tune. It was the one Tormund and I had danced to that time, over a year ago, when we still didn't know what each other was thinking or feeling.

Smiling, I rose to join him in a dance.

But instead of taking my hand, he knelt.

My breath shuddered out of me.

Gently, he took my hand, gazing up at me with so much adoration I could barely breathe. "Astrid Balstad. You know I adore you."

I swallowed the lump of sunstone in my throat. Heart beating madly, I nodded.

"You are my sun. My moon. The first thought in my head when I wake and the last before I sleep. And when you smile, the pieces of me that were broken feel whole again. I've told you before that I want to spend the rest of my life with you, but I want to do one better than that. I want to make binding vows with you. I want to stand before the gods and declare that you're mine. Astrid, will you marry me?"

Tears gushed down my face. I knew he loved me—he'd told me a thousand times. But I didn't think he'd want to make the vows, not the way dwarves did. Shadow demons had different gods and different customs. And yet here he was, giving me this one last thing. A thing I'd never asked, never wanted to pressure him to do.

I smiled through my tears. "Yes, Tormund. Of course, I'll marry you."

He wrapped his hands around my waist and lifted me into his arms, twirling me through the tavern and toward the dance floor. Cheers exploded in our wake, reminiscent of the competition's end.

But this win tasted far sweeter. It filled my heart with intoxicating hope for a future I'd once thought was a dream and nothing more. A happy life with the person who mattered most to me in this world. There would be hard days, yes, but we would face them together. And whatever might come our way, I believed we'd survive it.

I believed in *us*.

Next in the Falling for Fables world is...
Built by Magic
Preorder Now

Stay up-to-date with new releases in the *Falling for Fables* series by signing up to Jenna's newsletter.

GLOSSARY

DRAUGR - those who bond with dragons and channel their power

FENRIR - wolf-like creatures who can form powerful bonds with folk

FILDUR - the elemental magic of fire

FITTEST UNDER THE MOUNTAIN - a yearly competition in the dwarven mountains to find the fastest and strongest amongst them

FOLK - beings in tune with the Galdur; includes elves, orcs, pixies, trolls, fenrir, demons, giants, kraken, and dwarves

FREYA - the ancient goddess of the elements

GALDUR - the elemental magic that runs through the bones of the earth; can be controlled by rare sand

GEMSTONES - gems that are mined by the dwarves, some of which have magical properties, such as sunstones

JORDUR - the elemental magic of earth

MIDSUMMER GAMES - an annual celebration that takes place in Wyndale, complete with a tournament; the winner may ask for one gift from the island

THE OLD GODS - ancient beings who crafted the world and gifted the folk with Galdur

THOR - the God of Thunder, worshipped by the dwarves

VATNOR - the elemental magic of water

VINDUR - the elemental magic of air

YULE - the annual winter festival to celebrate harmony, bounty, and happiness, and to bless the coming year

ALSO BY JENNA WOLFHART

Falling for Fables

Forged by Magic

Brewed in Magic

Mined in Magic

Built by Magic

The Mist King

Of Mist and Shadow

Of Ash and Embers

Of Night and Chaos

Of Dust and Stars

The Fallen Fae

Court of Ruins

Kingdom in Exile

Keeper of Storms

Tower of Thorns

Realm of Ashes

Prince of Shadows (A Novella)

ABOUT THE AUTHOR

Jenna Wolfhart spends her days dreaming up stories about swoony fae kings and rugged blacksmiths. When she's not writing, she loves to deadlift, rewatch Game of Thrones, and drink far too much coffee.

Born and raised in America, Jenna now lives in England with her husband and her two dogs.

www.jennawolfhart.com
jenna@jennawolfhart.com
tiktok.com/@jennawolfhart